'I had a thought,' Lachlan said. 'It's a bit hard to find the right words, and I don't know that I'll be any good at it.' He paused. 'The fact is, we've had authorisation for a few months now to employ a nurse at Borragidgee in addition to myself and the Aboriginal health workers. So far we haven't been able to get anyone because they'd have to live in an old caravan. I thought, since you're not keen on Darwin, that you might like to take the post and come and live there, only not in the caravan. . .' he stopped and looked up, his blue eyes studying her searchingly with an expression Elspeth could not read '. . .but as my wife.'

She gazed at him in sheer amazement and he sat back suddenly. 'That would have to be the worst, most inept proposal ever made, wouldn't it?' he said disgustedly. 'I'm sorry. I said I'd be no good at it, and I've been out of civilisation too long. It's. . .it's. . .well, perhaps it's best to consider it as a practical business proposition, since we don't know each other too well.'

Lilian Darcy is Australian, but has recently married and now makes her home in New York. She writes for theatre, film and television as well as her romance fiction work, and her interests include winter sports, music, travel and the study of languages. Hospital volunteer work and friends in the medical profession provide the research background for her novels, which she enjoys writing because of the opportunity they give for creating realistic, modern stories, believable characters and a romance that will stand the test of time.

Previous Titles

UNWILLING PARTNERS
SISTER PAGE'S PAST

A PRACTICAL MARRIAGE

BY

LILIAN DARCY

MILLS & BOON LIMITED
ETON HOUSE   18–24 PARADISE ROAD
RICHMOND   SURREY   TW9 1SR

First published in Great Britain 1991
by Mills & Boon Limited

© Lilian Darcy 1991

Australian copyright 1991
Philippine copyright 1991
This edition 1991

ISBN 0 263 77178 4

Set in 10 on 11 pt Linotron Plantin
03-9103-58830
Typeset in Great Britain by Centracet, Cambridge
Made and printed in Great Britain

CHAPTER ONE

THE Rock Bar was a loud, crowded expanse of people, stretching, it seemed to Elspeth, as far as the eye could see in all directions. This was a bit of an illusion, of course. She and her friends were seated right in the middle of the place, with drinkers and flirters in groups of different sizes blocking any view of the street, or even of the bar itself, where harassed barmen and barmaids pulled constantly at beer taps.

Elspeth nodded and smiled at Jane, a nursing friend, giving every appearance of an attentive listener although she could hear only one word in three of Jane's energetically shouted anecdote. It concerned some kind of problem that had cropped up at the hospital today. . . Dr Jenkins. . .? Ward Twelve. . .?

'Anyway, don't you think I was right?' Jane demanded finally.

'Oh, yes! Oh, definitely,' Elspeth agreed with conviction. Clearly it was the expected response, and it was too difficult to admit that she hadn't heard properly.

Then Jane's attention was caught suddenly by a new arrival who had joined another loud group adjacent to Elspeth's own table.

'Oh, my goodness, there's Mark!' she exclaimed. 'I didn't think he'd be in town again so soon.'

She darted off, leaving Elspeth to her own devices. The other three nurses in the group were huddled together, involved in a conversation of their own. Elspeth sat there and drank a last half-hearted mouthful of her lemon squash. The ice had melted into the drink now, and it tasted watery. She glanced at the door. It was wet in several places with spilt beer. This wouldn't concern the owners of the Rock Bar, of course. The floor was made of bare concrete, and the tables of hard, plain jarrah wood, unadorned by such niceties as tablecloths. The bar was open on the sides to let cooling breezes through, a necessary function even in Darwin's coolest months, unless there was air-conditioning. The noise level seemed to be rising even higher as more and more people finished their Friday afternoon's work and came thirstily in quest of a cold beer.

Elspeth Moore hated the Rock Bar. In fact, if she admitted it honestly to herself, she hated Darwin. It was purely a personal response. She hadn't managed to 'click' with the small city, although so many other Southerners did. One of the reasons was that too many people drank entirely too much here. She didn't mind the odd glass of beer or wine herself, but that was as far as it went.

She looked at Kate, Sue and Rebecca. They seemed happy, animated and at home here at the Rock Bar, and they came here at least once a week. Was it just her own rather stuffy and snobbish Melbourne upbringing that made her unable to enjoy this place, with its reek of beer, its lack of comfort and its constant press of shouting drinkers? Surely not! Was it Melbourne's cool wet winters and warm dry summers that left her unprepared for the draining heat and humidity of the wet season which had just ended? This seemed more likely.

The main question was, what was she going to do about it? She had been here for six months. Could she possibly resign from her position on the men's medical ward of Darwin's Royal Northern Hospital and go back. . .slink back, really. . .to Melbourne? It didn't take long to answer this: no, she could not. She thought about all the reasons she had left Melbourne in the first place: the fact that she had turned thirty in November and had still not found the love she secretly dreamed of;

the fact that her mother's response to this embarrassing/ husbandless state was to propose yet another cocky, pompous and clean-cut lawyer—usually the son of a friend from a charity committee—as a blind date; the fact that she could see various friends and relatives starting to feel sorry for her, and this was the last thing she wanted, never having been someone who liked feeling sorry for herself, let alone inspiring that feeling in others.

How many of those gruelling barbecues and cocktail hours had her mother put her through last year? Four! No, it was *five*, Elspeth remembered with a sudden grin, thinking of her mother's tragi-comic expression when one particular man that she had carefully selected turned up at a Sunday lunch with a brand-new fiancé in tow. Poor Mums! She was sincerely trying, but seemed unable to learn that Elspeth simply didn't *like* clean-cut young lawyers and financiers, just didn't feel relaxed and at home with their talk of investment, portfolios, tax shelters and client wheeler-dealings. That was why she had broken her ten-month engagement to the first of them eight years ago at the age of twenty-two.

Since then, she had to admit, her attempts to come up with the kind of man she *did* like hadn't been conspicuously successful. There was that hospital orderly, whose idea of a scintillating evening was sitting in front of the television with a huge pile of take-away chips, flipping the channels every three minutes with his remote control. And then there was Frank, who had rescued her after a bicycle accident early last year. She had gone out with him for three months, but his hazy yet intense devotion to some of the wilder reaches of New Age spirituality, including something he called 'Atlantean Shamanism', had become a little off-putting after a while.

It was unfortunate that all her friends seemed to side with her mother. Many of them had married lawyers and financiers themselves—people their brothers had been at school or university with—and if a single man of similar ilk ever trespassed into their midst, hey presto! A dinner-party would be quickly manufactured and Elspeth would be told to get her chestnut hair done and wear a new dress. She felt bad about hating such evenings. All of these people were very nice, their marriages seemed happy, their lives seemed full, but when she tried to fit herself into such a life. . .she just didn't go.

Darwin had been partly an escape, she had to admit, but, more than that, it had been a genuine attempt to answer her mother's exasperated question, 'Well, what on earth is it that you *do* want?' Elspeth hadn't had an answer at the time, but then she had seen the advertisement, had applied, and had presented her mother with the news.

'This is what I want. Something a bit more. . .challenging.' It was hard to find the words. . . More real, more nitty-gritty.

Her mother had been appalled. Darwin? Bad enough being a nurse at all—such a messy, physical profession—but in a place like Darwin, full of tropical diseases and unnaturally large insects. . .

And now it seemed that like a child having got what she thought she wanted, Elspeth didn't like it after all and was well on way to proving Camilla Moore right. It was hardly surprising that she felt ashamed of herself, bewildered at her own feelings, and uncertain of what to do about them.

A diversion occurred at that moment, in the midst of these unproductive musings. Jane returned with Mark in tow, as well as an unknown bearded man who carried a tray containing a fresh round of drinks for all of them. Kate, Sue and Rebecca turned to the newcomers with interest, ready to abandon their previous conversation for the sake of studying some fresh faces.

Jane made the introductions. 'You've met Mark, haven't you, Kate? But I don't think the others have. Sue, Rebecca, Elspeth—all nurses with us at the hospital. Mark's a park ranger down at Walkadu, and this is Lachlan, who's a doctor. . .'

'*The* doctor,' Mark amended.

'. . .at Borragidgee,' Jane finished.

'Which is about fifty miles south-east of the park,' the medical man put in, with a deep voice and a strong trace of Scottish accent, apparently addressing himself mainly to Elspeth.

She nodded politely, with a smile, but in fact her attention was mainly on Mark and Jane. The latter was gazing up at the tall blond park ranger with the dewy expression that, in Jane, betokened a crush. Unfortunately, Mark's manner, although friendly towards Jane, didn't seem to indicate the same interest. Elspeth was disappointed. Clearly, Mark was the mystery man Jane had been hinting at for the past three months—wildly good-looking and really nice, she had said, but only in town every so often.

'What should I *do*?' Jane had wailed.

'Well, don't spend too much time thinking about him, for a start,' Elspeth had advised, 'or you'll only go silly and over-eager when you see him.'

'Yes, yes, you're right,' had been Jane's reply, but it now seemed clear that she hadn't been able to put this advice into practice.

Mark managed to find extra chairs and the two men sat down. Jane promptly shuffled her own chair closer to Mark and started telling him about her bad day at the hospital. His eyes strayed every now and then as he listened. Elspeth tried to forget about it—after all, it was Jane's problem—but she had a tendency to become too generously caught up in her friends' romantic trials, and she knew that Jane would demand 'feedback' after the evening was over—'Was I too silly? Was I a good listener? I went on too long about Dr Jenkins, I know that, but he seemed interested. . .'

Elspeth herself had always hated asking those sorts of questions or giving those sorts of details. It had been another of her problems in Melbourne. 'Come on, tell us about him, Ellie. What did you talk about at dinner? Did he kiss you?'

She became aware that Kate and Rebecca were asking the doctor—Lachlan, but last names had not been given—about his work at Borragidgee, and she managed to make herself listen. At first, she had had the impression that he was shy. With the full, reddish-brown beard that hid most of his face and the lean, almost gawky set of his tall figure, he looked like someone who was more at home in the quiet of a bush-town like Borragidgee than in the centre of the aggressive social scene at the Rock Bar. But now that he was being drawn out on a subject that interested him he became an animated speaker, gesturing with tanned, sinewy hands and gazing frankly at his questioners with blue eyes that were startlingly clear and bright against the strangely yellowed tan of his face.

No, Elspeth amended to herself, he wasn't just looking at Kate and Rebecca; he turned equally often towards herself, although she had said nothing to him yet. Actually, she liked that in a man—someone who made an effort to include everyone. Now he was drawing out quiet Sue, comparing his work to hers in the paediatric ward.

Elspeth decided that she must be getting used to the high decibel level of the Rock Bar, as it didn't seem so hard to hear now as it had been earlier. Just as she was actually starting to enjoy herself here, perhaps for the first time since her initiation visit with Jane and Kate back in November, two more nurses and a physiothera-pist called Stephen came past, caught sight of Kate, Sue and Rebecca, and were soon talking with them, shifting the girls' attention away from the circle of chairs that had been established before. Jane was still monopolising Mark, but perhaps he *did* seem pleased about it, Elspeth noted with satisfaction.

Lachlan whoever-he-was shrugged and grinned rue-fully at Elspeth, as if he too was disappointed that their talk about the work at Borragidgee had ended, and now, suddenly, it began to seem again as if he was shy after all. Or quiet, anyway. Reserved and reticent. He looked tired, too, she noticed suddenly, and that odd colour to his face in spite of his heavy tan, didn't come from healthy, iron-rich blood pulsing beneath. She had a sudden, nurse-like desire to ask him if he felt all right, and to suggest a succession of early nights and vitamin pills. Of course, though, he was a doctor himself, quite capable of assessing his own condition. Perhaps he'd just had a frenetic few days.

There was silence between them for quite some time. Elspeth's mind went blank, as it sometimes did on such occasions—with the lawyers, it had happened often. She felt desperately that it was up to her to introduce a suitable subject, and consquently could think of nothing at all.

'Do you like it here?' Lachlan was the one, finally, to fill the breach.

'Do you mean Darwin,' she queried, 'or the Rock Bar?'

'Well, both. Either.'

'Darwin's fine,' she lied, then felt impelled to be at least partly honest in her response. 'But I loathe the Rock Bar.'

'Me too,' he said cheerfully, his Scottish accent strong. He looked around for a moment, his bright eyes narrowed. Then he laughed, a rich, cheerful sound. 'I wonder what an alien visitor would think on stepping out of a space-craft and seeing this place,' he said. 'Probably that it was some kind of punishment cell, not a place where people came for pleasure.'

Elspeth laughed, then silence fell between them again, and her attention was caught by Mark leading Jane over to meet another friend with—a good sign—an arm around her shoulders. One thing that had to be said in the Rock Bar's favour was that you certainly met a lot of people here. Five minutes later, she finished her drink.

'Want to go somewhere else?' Lachlan said suddenly, having seen her empty glass.

Elspeth started guiltily. Her mind had gone back to the question of her future in Darwin, and she had almost forgotten the bearded doctor's presence.

'Oh. Yes. I suppose so,' she said clumsily, looking involuntarily at the others.

But it soon seemed that he didn't mean to invite the others. He stood up and reached out a lean hand to Elspeth, who took it because it was there and let him help her to her feet. His hand was surprisingly cool and dry, a pleasure in this town of sticky bodies. Then he touched Mark briefly on the shoulder.

'I'm off,' he said. 'And so's Elspeth. See you later.'

'Right-oh.' Mark nodded indifferently.

Elspeth noted that all the others were unaware that she was leaving, and decided that goodbyes would be too intrusive. She would see half of them at the hospital on her 'A' shift tomorrow morning anyway.

Outside, a breeze struck, cool and fresh on her face and body, a reminder of how hot it had been in the middle of the press of bodies. It was still only just after six o'clock, and quite light. In the bar, it had felt later.

'There's that place down by the water,' Lachlan

suggested. 'It's much nicer, don't you think? We can sit outside. Catch the sunset.'

'We'll have to be quick,' Elspeth pointed out. So near the Equator, Darwin's sunsets were rapid affairs, pretty—especially over the water—but with none of the lingering splendours of light that glorified the day's end in higher latitudes.

'Do you have a car?' he asked.

'Yes,' she nodded, flourishing the Mazda keys she had just taken from her bag.

'So do I,' he said. 'That's silly, isn't it? Will we go separately?'

After a bit of awkward negotiation they chose to take Elspeth's car. This was a secret relief to her, as, after all, she barely knew the man, and you always felt more in control in your own vehicle. She would drop him back at the Toyota four-wheel drive he pointed out in the car park after their sunset drink.

But in fact it wasn't after just a drink when she found herself back in the Rock Bar car park, it was at eleven o'clock, and she couldn't quite understand where the evening had gone. Perhaps her watch was wrong, she thought, looking at it for the first time since leaving the Rock Bar five hours ago. She started the Mazda's engine again. Lachlan McLintock, whose last name she had found out several hours earlier, was just climbing into the high driver's seat of his Toyota. She waved at him one last time and then shook her left wrist and lifted it to her ear. The ticking of her watch sounded quite normal.

As she drove down the now quiet streets back to the hospital, she tried to work out how the time had passed so quickly. They had had a hock, lime and soda each; they had gone for a shallow splash along the water's edge to cool their feet; they had talked about all sorts of things, but she couldn't for the life of her remember much about what those things were.

Lachlan had suggested dinner, and her stomach had said it was a good idea. The nurses' home meal-hour would be long over. He knew of a Vietnamese restaurant with outside tables and they had sat there on the quiet pavement, just a few other couples and foursomes around them, eating a deliciously fragrant meal of spring rolls, chicken and fish and talking about. . .again, she couldn't recreate the conversation in her mind. It seemed to have covered so much ground, and with none of the long tales of their own professional prowess and cunning that her mother's selected lawyers had always been so full of. In fact, he hadn't talked much about himself at all.

In the car park back at the Rock Bar he had touched her hand in farewell. 'You live at the nurses' home, right?'

'Yes.'

Then he had just nodded and opened his car door. She wasn't disappointed that he hadn't kissed her. After all, they'd only just met. More importantly, she had already decided that physically he wasn't her type. The beard, for one thing, redder than his shock of rather unkempt dark hair, his lean—skinny!—almost gawky frame, for another. An unfair decision, perhaps, since he seemed such a nice person, but if The Spark wasn't there, it just wasn't there, and there was nothing you could do about it—or so various friends and various magazines had always assured her.

'When it happens,' Cousin Amanda had said in Melbourne three years ago, 'you'll know. You'll just *know*. I did. Immediately.'

Of course, Cousin Amanda was divorced now, but that hadn't changed her opinion on The Spark that had to happen. Well, unfortunately it hadn't happened for Elspeth tonight.

Two weeks later she was beginning to wonder if it was fair of her to keep on seeing Lachlan. Getting ready in her room for another Friday-night meal, she counted up and realised that this was the fifth time they had been out together now, including that first evening and a quickly snatched lunch.

Well, it couldn't last much longer. She wasn't sure of the exact timing but she knew he must be returning to Borragidgee soon. He had been ill, it turned out, although he hadn't mentioned what was wrong, and she hadn't liked to ask. This stay in Darwin was an attempt to recuperate away from the demands of his patients, which he could never manage to ignore at Borragidgee, even when he needed to for his own well-being. And she herself wanted to take her mid-year holidays in Melbourne some time soon. She had two weeks due. Perhaps she should put in the leave request form on Monday. . .

Tonight, then, might end up being their last evening together. In fact, it ought to be, and even if he suggested another date, she would politely turn him down. Accordingly, she decided to dress especially well for the evening as a tribute to the fact that she really did like him so much, and so that he wouldn't think she had only been stringing him along, careless of his feelings.

Not, she recalled abruptly and a little shamefacedly, that she had any good reason to think he was serious and smitten. He still hadn't kissed her. In fact, she now realised, there had been no suggestion at all on his part that he wanted anything more than friendliness and companionship during his brief stay in Darwin.

Studying herself in the mirror and putting down the brown mascara she had been brushing on to her already thick lashes, Elspeth found that she was blushing.

'Am I being a fool?' she questioned her reflection. 'I *am*! Oh, no! I really am!'

It was only silly, shallow self-flattery that had made her think he was pursuing her with a romantic intent. Had he detected the self-satisfied attitude she now realised had been colouring her thoughts? Working out the correct answer to this question seemed to be a matter of surprising urgency, and she stood motionless and unseeing in front of the mirror for nearly ten minutes, reviewing her own conduct, and his. Somehow, it would be absolutely awful if he had guessed how smug she had been. . .

Finally she was able to decide that she had been over-reacting with these fears. For both of them, it was a pleasant friendship, and this was the only attitude she had ever betrayed. Fortunately she had said nothing about him to her friends, either. They hadn't quite registered the fact that she had gone off with him that first Friday, and since then Jane, at least, had been absorbed in her own problems.

'Mark's only flirting with me,' she had concluded to Elspeth last week, and now Mark had returned to Walkadu and Jane was pining.

Elspeth resumed work on her make-up. The earth-toned smudging of shadow on her eyelids complemented her colouring, and the bright red lipstick she now carefully applied made a bold note that echoed the scarlet of her simple silk dress with its spaghetti straps and crisp, figure-hugging fabric. She had brought the dress up from Melbourne—it was one of the items in her wardrobe that had been bought for one of Mrs Moore's cocktail parties—but this was the first time she had worn it up here. The vivid colour showed off the light, cream-gold tan of her skin and contrasted with the dark brown hair she wore swept into a high ponytail by a frivolous scarlet clip.

A slim gold chain around her neck echoed the many golden and chestnut highlights in her hair, and her brown eyes glowed warmly in a face that was dotted on nose and cheeks with tiny freckles. A small red mesh bag and open-toed shoes completed her outfit. The latter's heels augmented her already above-average height and gave her the grace and proportions of a fashion model, although perhaps she was too big-boned for today's over-slim stereotype.

Elspeth herself didn't have quite the confidence in her appearance that others told her she should have. Those freckles! She had hated them for as long as she could remember, having been teased about them during school days when they had been more numerous. And she had always secretly longed to be more petite. But it was good to know, having made her best effort to look nice, that Lachlan wouldn't be planning an evening at the Rock Bar.

Time to go already. She hurried downstairs to the foyer of the nurses' home and Lachlan was waiting there, holding flowers.

'Oh, dear, bad choice,' he said, glancing down at them as he handed them to her.

'Never mind,' she said. 'I'll put them in my room, shall I? They'll go with the pink bedspread and give the place a lovely lift, even if they clash with this dress.'

She took the lavish bunch which was dominated by pink rosebuds and blue-mauve ageratum that both clashed violently with her scarlet dress, and hurried back up the two flights of stairs, finding an old coffee-jar from the kitchenette near her room and arranging the flowers in it quickly. Hopefully she wouldn't have to mention that she couldn't grace the flowers with a vase.

Back in the foyer, she saw that he was looking admiringly at her outfit. 'I'm glad you're dressed up,' he said with his deep Scottish burr, 'because we're going to the Grange.' It was Darwin's newest and most expensive restaurant.

Nodding and giving the right exclamation of delight, Elspeth began to feel a foreboding certainty that the evening was going to take an unexpected turn.

Two hours later she had lost this suspicion, caught up only in each pleasurable moment of eating and talking. It was disappointing, somehow, that she seemed to find friendship with a man so much easier than romance. Surely that wasn't how it ought to be! It wasn't that she lacked a strong sensuous element to her inner make-up, either. . .

'Penny for your thoughts,' he said, breaking the silence in which this last musing had come to her.

'Oh, I couldn't!' she gasped, without stopping to censor her words, then bit her lip. What would he. . .?

He laughed, the deep, frank sound that she liked and had heard often over these past two weeks. 'Serve me right,' he said. 'It's an awful question, and there should be a fine for asking it. People always say it to me when I'm thinking the most banal, ridiculous thing.'

'Yes, that's right, isn't it?' she said, grateful for this way out of her *faux pas*. 'Me too.'

Silence fell again. They were sipping coffee and liqueurs accompanied by tiny chilled morsels of dark chocolate. He coughed behind a lean hand, then spoke. 'I have to go back to Borragidgee on Sunday, Ellie,' he said. She had told him about this often-used shortening of her name and he had dropped into it naturally. The name sounded nice in his deep, accented tones.

'Oh, do you?' she said. 'Yes, I thought you must be due back there soon.' She was making herself speak lightly, but—even though she had half expected this announcement—it had created a greater feeling of let-down and disappointment inside her than she had been prepared for. She added, 'As it happens, I'm hoping for some time away from Darwin soon, too. Perhaps in Melbourne.' It was an attempt to sound casual about their respective plans. She realised that in many ways she would miss him. . .

'Are you?' he said mechanically, not sounding as if it mattered much. 'Melbourne? To see your family?'

'Yes.'

'Looking forward to it, I suppose,' he conjectured, 'since you're not all that keen on Darwin.'

She had confessed this to him a week ago, after her initial lie on the subject at the Rock Bar.

'Unfortunately Melbourne's got its problems too,' she put in now.

'Oh yes,' he nodded. 'Your mother and your friends and the lawyer lifestyle.'

Good heavens! Elspeth thought. I really have told him a lot, haven't I? She had forgotten about her Melbourne confessions, made one night over supper after a movie. Silence fell again for a moment.

'I had a thought,' he said. 'It's a bit hard to find the right words, and I don't know that I'll be any good at it.' He paused. 'That fact is, we've had authorisation for a few months now to employ a nurse at Borragidgee in addition to myself and the Aboriginal health workers. So far we haven't been able to get anyone because they'd have to live in an old caravan. The five applicants all backed out when they heard that, understandably, and the situation is getting a bit critical, especially since the new person will need a special permit. The town is on Aboriginal land, you see. I thought, since you're not keen on Darwin, that you might like to take the post and come and live there, only not in the caravan. . .' he stopped and looked up, his blue eyes studying her searchingly with an expression she could not read '. . .but as my wife.'

CHAPTER TWO

ELSPETH had the odd realisation that, even though Lachlan's proposal came as a complete surprise to her conscious mind, her unconscious, intuitive self had been expecting it. She also had the odd, *very* odd, feeling that—even while her brain whirled with a dozen reasons why it was impossible, why she should be, perhaps, outraged at the casual, practical way he had said it, why it was the last thing in the world she would consider doing—at some point in the future, she was going to accept.

No, you're not, another part of herself asserted with far more firmness. You don't love him, and you'd better tell him so straight away. . .if you can find the words.

He sensed her hesitation and came in quickly again. 'The house is nice, and the town. It's got an all-weather airstrip. . .'

She gazed at him in sheer amazement and he sat back suddenly. 'That would have to be the worst, most inept proposal of marriage ever made, wouldn't it?' he said disgustedly. 'I'm sorry. I said I'd be no good at it, and I've been out of civilisation for too long. It's. . .it's. . .well, perhaps it's best to consider it as a practical business proposition, since we don't know each other too well.' Oddly this suggestion came as a relief to Elspeth. She hadn't wanted a passionate declaration of love from him.

He went on. 'Let's not talk about feelings. The fact is, there really is no decent accommodation for a nurse, except at my place, and I wouldn't want the community to get the impression that their doctor would bring in a new nurse just to have an affair with her. . ."shack up with her," as people would say. When you said you didn't like Darwin, and didn't want to go back to Melbourne, the job seemed like a way out for you. . .as well as for me, but. . .you're angry, aren't you? Would you like to go home?'

He stood up abruptly, his height coming as a surprise to her as it often did. Was it her imagination or did he look less gaunt and thin than he had done two weeks ago?

'No, I'm not angry,' she said, unable to frame the words of rejection. 'I understand that it's a difficult situation for you.'

She *did* understand too. Before coming to Darwin six months ago she might not have done, but life up in the Top End, as it was called by locals, was different. In an isolated community, where distances were vast between neighbouring towns, companionship was important and opportunities for finding it were rare. People were thrust into quick decisions made on a hunch, social conventions were adapted to answer to different needs. She sensed that Lachlan had disliked the circumstances of his proposal almost more than she herself had done, sensed also that behind the awkward words had lain a genuine desire to find a solution to both their problems, albeit an unusual one.

'Don't answer now, then,' he came in quickly. 'Don't give any kind of answer unless it's a definite and categorical "no". If you think you could consider it, take time to think while you're in Melbourne, say, if you go. And if we do get married and it doesn't work out. . . I hate to say it, Ellie, but there's always divorce.'

'I don't suppose many people discuss getting married and getting divorced in the same breath.' Elspeth laughed. She couldn't say, 'no', bluntly to his face like that, and seized on 'thinking it over' as a way out.

Perhaps over the phone. . . No, that was cowardly. For now it seemed that a light-hearted approach was the best way to ease the tension that hovered over their table.

'Probably in Hollywood they do,' he answered her previous comment, 'with their pre-nuptial agreements.'

'Oh, you've heard of Hollywood out there at Borragidgee, have you?' Elspeth quipped, and somehow the subject of marriage lapsed and wasn't referred to again.

An hour later they left the restaurant and began the journey back to the nurses' home in Lochlan's four-wheel drive. She noted that it was fitted out very much in keeping with the vehicle of an outback doctor, including the two-way radio set bolted to the roof just above her head. Having made his observation of her surroundings, she started to think about tomorrow. Would he suggest they see each other for his last day in Darwin? Probably. A boating trip perhaps. Should she accept? She didn't know. That proposal of his might hang in the air between them, making things awkward in the cold light of day.

Lachlan was driving steadily in silence. Perhaps he was thinking about these things too. . .

Then suddenly as they approached an intersection, cruising at a safe speed through their green light, a car shot out at them from the right, shattering the peace of the evening and the train of their thoughts. Before Elspeth was fully aware of what was happening Lachlan had swung the wheel of the four-wheel drive sharply to the left, uttering some violent, incomprehensible sounds. He couldn't be quick enough, however. The battered car came at them, also swerving, and swiped them roughly along the side with a hideous crash and a crunch of metal and glass. At this point Elspeth buried her face in her hands.

Their vehicle was still and quiet when she was able to

look up. The engine and bodywork both ticked as if settling back into their own shapes after being squeezed and distorted. The menacing column of a tall concrete lamp-post was pressed up against the passenger door. For a moment its significance didn't sink in, then Ellie realised just how close she had come to potentially serious injury. Her seatbelt too had helped to preserve her life.

Now she was able to focus on Lachlan McLintock and, horrified, she saw that he was slumped over the wheel. Motionless. A moan of fear was wrenched from her lips and, forgetting her professional training, she reached a hand to his strong, thin shoulder and almost shook him, squeezing and massaging with her hand as if his body was precious to her.

'Lachlan! Lachlan! His name was all she could say and then, to her intense, gut-weakening relief, he spoke.

'I'm all right, Ellie. Just limp.'

She breathed an incoherent prayer of thanks, then before she could touch him again, as she knew she wanted to—just to reassure herself that his skin really was warm and heathily pulsing beneath her fingers—he sat upright. His face was deathly pale, she saw, but his jaw was square and hard beneath the full beard.

'The people in the other car. . .' he said, and had opened the door before Elspeth had even remembered in her shock that there was another car.

She followed his gaze and saw the still, jagged outline of wreckage. The other vehicle had not been so lucky. It was crumpled against a lamp-post just like the one beyond Ellie's door, and broken glass made a glistening carpet like frost crystals all over the road.

'Go and see what you can do,' Lachlan said to her quickly and almost abruptly. 'I'll radio the hospital to send an ambulance.'

He saw that the lamp-post had penned her in and he

stood aside, holding the driver's door so that Elspeth could slide across and climb to the ground. The hand he offered her, and which she grabbed at gladly, was hard with tension and icy cold. Did her own feel the same to him? As soon as she was out he reached for the radio microphone, flipped a couple of switches and Elspeth heard him begin to speak into it as she raced towards the other car.

It felt as if minutes had elapsed since the screeching of tyres had ceased but Ellie knew hazily in the back of her mind that this was an illusion. A car had stopped safely off the edge of the road behind Lachlan's vehicle, and two more cars were being parked near the cross-street, where the traffic lights were only just turning amber again after the green signal that the careening, battered old vehicle she was heading towards now had not waited for.

A stranger approached the scene. 'Can we do anything?'

'I'm a nurse,' Ellie said, at last finding some professional assurance. 'I'm going to look. My. . .friend is a doctor. He's calling for an ambulance.' The stranger, a plump man in his late forties, fell into step awkwardly behind Ellie.

When she got to the car she knew immediately, and with a sick heart that the ambulance would be needed. More than one. There were three bodies in the car and a fourth seemed to have been flung clear. None of these people, all tragically young, were moving. The reek of alcohol came strongly through the shattered windscreen and side windows and among the debris flung across the car's bonnet Ellie saw a bottle of whisky, lidless and still dripping the last of its contents over the shabby red paintwork. Ironically it hadn't even been broken in the smash.

She heard a groan from inside the vehicle and then

saw that the young man who had been flung across the bonnet and on to the ground had his eyes open.

'Don't move him,' she told the middle-aged man who had been first on the scene with her.

But she approached the young man quickly, seeing that he was bleeding heavily from somewhere on his torso. His shirt was already soaked with blood. Lifting it and undoing three lower buttons with careful speed, she found the place and pressed her fingers into the wound, stemming the flow of blood to a slow seepage.

It was all she could do, but it was important. Back injury, internal organ damage. . .potentially fatal but not her concern. If the loss of blood wasn't stemmed first, that was what would kill him. Why, oh, *why*, she asked herself bitterly and angrily, did people drink and drive? Why, for so many men, was alcohol consumption a symbol of manhood? This boy—he only looked about seventeen—might never know a full, healthy manhood now.

A couple of other people had approached by this time with offers of help, and then Elspeth heard Lachlan's Scottish-lilted voice: 'Stand clear, everyone; the ambulances are on their way and should be here in a minute or two. The hospital's not far, thank God.'

Elspeth couldn't tell what he was doing with the other injured teenagers. Her own task was clear and fixed and left her no room for idly looking about. Quickly her fingers became cramped and her shoulder-blades ached from the awkward crouching position she had to hold. It seemed like more than the minute or two Lachlan had promised before the ambulance siren could at last be heard, getting nearer and louder rapidly.

After this, for what seemed like a long time, events were blurred and chaotic in Ellie's mind. The red flashes of the first ambulance, and then a second and third, and the blue flashes of two police cars coloured the scene in an erratic merry-go-round of light, and the crowd of onlookers—some merely ghoulish, others with a genuine desire to help—was a haze of shapes and sounds in the background.

Opinions about each youth's condition came to her in dribs and drabs from Lachlan and from the ambulance officers. Her own patient, whose blood still stickied her hands, looked like a hopeful case although the blood loss was severe. The driver of the car, on the other hand, would be lucky to survive. The third youth had a suspected spinal injury and the fourth might be able to leave hospital as early as next week. With further irony it seemed that this latter patient had been in an alcoholic stupor at the time of the accident and his consequent utter relaxation had helped to save his body from more severe injury.

The whole thing was a tragic, terrible mess, and Ellie began to have time to think of each teenager's family and the awful phone-call or police visit that would reach those families soon. . .

More time passed. Someone told her to hold out her hands and rub them together, and she felt cold water being poured on to them from a bottle. For a moment she didn't know what it was for; then she remembered the blood and scrubbed at her hands thoroughly so that her skin was pink and clean and throbbing before seizing the towel that was also offered and rubbing them dry. Looking up she found it was the middle-aged man who had first arrived on the scene.

'The police want to talk to you as well, love,' he said.

'Thank you very much,' she murmured mechanically, and then found a uniformed officer poised in front of her with a notebook and a barrage of questions about her name, address, occupation, and what she had seen, 'in her own words'. Vaguely, as she began her hesitant account, Elspeth wondered who else's words she could possibly have chosen.

Now at last the scene had quietened down. The onlookers had departed, the two witnesses to the accident had been questioned and the police barricades set up earlier around the area were being removed. Lachlan appeared. It seemed to Elspeth like hours since she had last seen him, and when he reached out his arms to her she almost fell into them, weakened and trembling at the warm strength of his body against hers and the press of his lips and bearded chin against her hair.

'You two be all right to get home on your own?' a policeman asked, breaking into the moment.

'Ellie?' Lachlan said, his voice even deeper than usual and with a throaty burr in it that emphasised his Scottish accent.

'I'm all right,' she said. Why had her teeth begun to chatter? It was cool but not cold. 'You're driving. Are *you* all right?'

'Yes, I'm fine.' He was still holding her, and Elspeth found it so comforting that she had no desire to move away.

The policeman seemed satisfied with their condition. 'Don't rush yourselves though,' he said. 'And you'll be hearing from us some time.'

'All right, officer.' Lachlan nodded and watched the policeman absently as he strode over to the official car, whose blue lights were still revolving silently. Then he said, 'You're shaking, Ellie. . .'

'I know; I'm sorry.'

'Don't apologise. My God, I'm shaking too, aren't I?'

'Yes, I suppose you are.'

'I feel quite chilly too.'

'Well, this is a chilly night. For Darwin.'

'That's right,' he laughed. 'For Darwin. It'd count as

a balmy afternoon where I come from, but everything's relative. I've got used to the heat now.'

'I hope I do.'

Their chatter was becoming meaningless and compulsive. Lachlan suddenly pulled her closer and again Ellie felt a sweet sense of comfort and safety and warmth at being in his arms. He was pressing his lips to her forehead now, and to her cheeks.

'Ellie, do marry me, do. Come to Borragidgee. Please!'

And all at once it sounded like the most wonderful idea in the world—to prolong this feeling of safety and warmth into a whole way of life, to have an answer for her future.

'All right,' she said almost feverishly, winding her arms more tightly around him. She forgot that at their first meeting she had thought him too thin. His shape and strength and hardness felt good against her; a sensation that was pure comfort and delight mingled with strong sensuality, and awareness began to fill her like hot, sweet liquid. With his lips just a finger's width from her own, she whispered, 'Yes, I will marry you. I will.' Her last two words were drowned in his kiss.

Elspeth rang her mother, Camilla, and her father, the successful stockbroker Charles Moore, the next morning. She told the story of the accident first. This was silly, really. Since she hadn't been hurt, and since it hadn't been her car, there was no reason for her mother ever to know about it; but somehow, after a narrow escape like that, she had the urge to reassure her parents. 'Don't worry. I'm all right. I'm alive and I wasn't hurt.'

Camilla Moore's fastidious reaction was an unfortunate reminder of Elspeth's own feelings. 'I told you it'd be ghastly up there with so much drunkenness.' It came as a petulant wail over the crackling line.

This note had been creeping increasingly into her

mother's voice over the years Elspeth realised, seemingly
in proportion to her father's increasing success. She felt
a sudden spurt of sympathy and tenderness for Mums.
Perhaps she wasn't as happy with the high-flying money-
orientated lifestyle as she always pretended to herself.

Mrs Moore's next words cooled the sympathy a little.

'So when are you resigning and coming home?'

'I'm not coming home, Mums.'

It was always Camilla Moore's response: if you find
something a little difficult, avoid it. Run away. It was a
response Elspeth was determined not to imitate.

'But we've got some people coming over next week,
and they're bringing their son, Paul. With a very good
firm in Perth and doing very——'

'I'm sorry, but I can't be there, Mums. I'm coming
down for a holiday in two or three weeks, but. . .you
see, what I really phoned you for is to tell you. . . I'm
engaged.'

It didn't seem real, of course, even during the ten
minutes of strenuous explanations she had to give to each
of her startled parents.

'You don't sound as happy about it as I thought you
would,' Camilla said reproachfully at one point.

'Of course I'm happy,' Elspeth answered rather too
heartily.

She had certainly been happy last night, weak and
swooning with happiness; and when Lachlan had taken
her in his arms and kissed her lingeringly she hadn't
seemed to mind about the beard nearly as much as she
would have expected. Or at least she couldn't remember
minding about it.

Today, though, she wasn't as sure of her feelings, and
could hardly remember the sensation of his kiss. A
curtain of confusion and haziness had been flung down
over the whole accident and its aftermath. It couldn't be
that she actually loved Lachlan, and it certainly couldn't

be that he loved her. The word had not been mentioned, and she had eaten a perfectly hearty breakfast this morning. . . Cousin Amanda in Melbourne hadn't eaten for a week after her engagement. It was odd that it seemed to get harder to know your own feelings as you got older. Surely it should get easier with greater maturity! And being a nurse of nine years' standing, who was thoroughly capable and competent in her professional world, should help as well, but it didn't.

Those of her friends who had got married at twenty or twenty-one had behaved like Cinderella or Juliet, floating in clouds of self-absorbed ecstasy for months as they had planned their bouquets and bridal parties, their guest lists and kitchenware.

But no, this was different, Elspeth reminded herself. Nothing had been said about love at all. Over dinner, Lachlan had called it business, and had mentioned divorce if it didn't work. The fact that neither of them had focused on the practical aspect of it in each other's arms after the accident wasn't significant. She might pretend to others that it was a love-match—too many questions would be asked otherwise—but it was foolish to try and deceive herself. The job sounded interesting, Lachlan was nice, and Elspeth's emotions had been worn down to the point where, at thirty years and six months, she was prepared to take a reasonable offer, so to speak, rather than holding out for her original rosy-edged price. She and Lachlan respected each other. That was probably a better basis than most kinds of love, anyway.

No admitting that to Mums, of course. 'It doesn't sound as if you've known him very long, darling, if you don't even know where he's from in Scotland,' Camilla Moore said.

'I didn't need to know him for long,' Elspeth said. 'It. . .it just happened.'

After some more awkwardly dropped bombshells—

that there wouldn't be a big Melbourne wedding, that there would be a simple ceremony in a tiny wooden church in Borragidgee, and that Mums wouldn't be able to meet Lachlan until the ceremony since he couldn't get down to Melbourne—Elspeth put down the phone. She was meeting Lachlan at noon for a boating picnic and it was time to start getting ready.

A fellow nurse, an acquaintance only, who was making herself a cup of coffee in the tiny kitchenette that adjoined the sitting-room, looked across curiously. 'Did I hear you tell your mother you're getting married?'

'Yes.' Pointless to attempt secrecy. She would have to start telling her close friends this evening.

'And he's a doctor. . . Congratulations!'

'That's not why I'm marrying him,' Elspeth said defensively.

'Oh, no! Of course not! I didn't mean. . .' Nurse Evans looked a little taken aback and Ellie realised that her own doubts had coloured her response in an odd way. Suddenly she was very nervous at the thought of seeing Lachlan in half an hour and she didn't quite know why. Was she afraid she was going to change her mind? Or afraid that *he* was? Perhaps she was most afraid that neither of them would back out and the whole thing would actually become a reality! Surely when she saw him it would become clear. . .

But she didn't see him. Just as she had finished changing into a blue denim skirt and boldly-patterned jungle-print blouse, there was a knock at her bedroom door and it was Celia Evans again.

'There's a phone-call for you,' she said, and Elspeth hurried to the sitting-room. She wasn't expecting the strange woman's voice that spoke.

'Hello, this is Barbara Johnson.'

'Who?'

'Barbara Johnson, the flying bishop's wife.'

It became clear eventually. Anglican bishop David Johnson piloted his own small aircraft in order to keep in touch with his far-flung parishioners, and he was on his way to Borragidgee now. Apparently there had been some trouble there last night, a fight, and Lachlan needed to return as well to give medical treatment and, it seemed, to calm the agitated feelings in the small community. He was going with David Johnson in the bishop's plane, and someone would drive his Toyota back to Borragidgee within the next few days.

'But he's left a message for you,' Barbara Johnson said a little distractedly. In the background, Elspeth could hear children playing loudly and the barking of a dog. 'He says if you could go to the Darwin Flying Doctor Base at six o'clock this evening, he'll radio in so you can talk. He says he'll understand if you've changed your mind, and that you'll know what he's referring to.'

After thanks from Elspeth and a few more harassed words from Barbara Johnson, the call came to an end, leaving Elspeth more uncertain than ever about the way events were overtaking her.

It seemed a long time until six o'clock and she couldn't settle to anything during the afternoon. She went to check on the progress of last night's accident victims, and found that even the most seriously injured youth would at least survive, thanks to prompt and intensive surgery. She wrote out her resignation from the hospital, able to give just two weeks' notice because of the holidays she had been planning to take in any case. Then she simply drifted about until it was time to leave for the RFDS Base.

The drive out to the base was a pleasant one, although for the first five minutes she was hampered by nerves after last night's near miss in Lachlan's car. It was early May, a month of relatively cool days and nights when vegetation was still lush from the rains that had ended a month ago. On first arriving in Darwin Elspeth had been amazed at the rapid, fertile growth around the city's houses and parks, but now she was used to it. She wished she knew more about the colourful, luxuriant plants and flowers that she saw, but her horticultural knowledge was limited to the English-style rose gardens and bulb beds of her parents' wealthy suburb.

It was difficult to believe that the ladylike—some said spinsterish—yet unhappy Melbourne girl she once had been could now be driving out to a Flying Doctor base to confirm over the radio the details of her impending marriage to a man she had known for only two weeks. . .

Then, as she thought this, and thought of the clumsy, ill-fitting figure she had cut in her parents' world, she knew a sudden rush of happiness. It was weird. It was as unlike the tame engagement to a rising lawyer that had been the destiny lying in wait for her in Melbourne as it could possibly be, but my goodness, it was already infinitely more interesting! She laughed aloud and banished all doubts—temporarily, at least.

At the base she was welcomed at once by a fellow nurse who clearly knew who she was and led her immediately into the radio room.

Lachlan's voice sounded unfamiliar over the radio transmitter. 'Are you there, Ellie? Over.'

'Yes, I am. Over.'

'It's Lachlan.' He must be as nervous as she suddenly was. 'Are you still. . .? I mean, do you still want to. . .? You know what I mean.' His 'Over!' contained a note of impatience both at his own awkwardness and at the awkwardness of two-way radio as a means of personal communication. They were both aware that a dozen other people could and would be listening in.

'I haven't changed my mind,' Elspeth answered him as clearly and firmly as she could.

'Good!' It was matter of fact. 'And the date we talked about is still all right?'

'Yes, it should be.'

After this they were able to be more open as they arranged more of the details. They didn't waste time in idle chat. It simply seemed too hard. Elspeth sat back from the complex transmitter equipment in the end and smiled at the radio operator a little helplessly.

'Nice little church they've got at Borragidgee now,' he said. His calm acceptance of the situation in contrast to her mother's appalled response gave Elspeth some further reassurance.

'Congratulations and good luck. He's a gorgeous man,' said the young nurse with warm sincerity as she farewelled Elspeth in the doorway.

This wasn't the response she got in Melbourne two weeks later. Her last fortnight at Royal Northern had passed easily enough, with much curiosity about her surprise news but only warm wishes and genuine support from her friends. Lachlan had written to her twice, the first time to express in a reserved, unflowery sort of way how confident he felt about their decision, and how he would do everything to try and make her happy at Borragidgee. The second letter, she was surprised and touched to find, contained a generous cheque, 'for the trip to Melbourne, and for a wedding dress. Whatever you choose, it will look beautiful.'

Camilla Moore didn't have quite the same confidence. She and Elspeth toured Melbourne's bridal shops together, but the beaded satins, hooped petticoats and eight-foot trains that she fell in love with—'After all, it's a church wedding, darling!'—only made Elspeth feel uncomfortable and unhappy. She had a good idea of what kind of a church it would be and could imagine the state of the ground outside, too. No place for a satin train, definitely. As well, she wanted to fit in with the people of Borragidgee, not create the impression that a princess had come to live in their midst.

On her third shopping expedition, which she made alone, Elspeth found the dress she wanted. It had an ivory silk underdress that came to her slim calves, and an over-skirt and elbow-sleeved bodice in spidery lace of an unusual scalloped pattern. The dress flattered her slim figure and was formal enough for a church without being too inappropriately ostentatious for Borragidgee.

Her cousin Amanda was given the privilege of seeing the dress and pronounced herself disappointed in it, in the wedding itself, and in the choice of groom.

'After all this time,' she said, opening round blue eyes widely and flicking a strand of newly-bleached hair off her shoulder, 'I mean. . . I don't mean to be rude about this, I'm sure he's very nice, but I thought you'd pick someone really special.'

'Lachlan *is* special,' Elspeth said stoutly. She had wondered about confiding some of her qualms to Amanda, who was almost her own age, but she definitely wouldn't now.

'I meant *really* special,' Amanda insisted. 'I thought you'd go overseas and meet some famous exotic foreigner.'

'Lachlan *is* foreign. He's Scottish.'

'Oh well,' Amanda shrugged, 'if there's The Spark. . . You do look as if you're in love.'

'Do I?' Elspeth blurted in astonishment, wondering at the back of her mind why Amanda seemed to get younger in her mannerisms as the years went by. When they were both twenty Amanda had seemed astonishingly sophisticated and mature, and Elspeth had always felt gauche and babyish in comparison.

'Well, yes,' Amanda was saying, 'you do.'

'Oh.'

'What do you mean, "Oh"?'

'I just. . .didn't think it showed,' Elspeth explained lamely.

Cousin Amanda had been disappointed and horrified at the honeymoon plans, too. Basically, there wasn't going to be one. At least, not in the foreseeable future, given Lachlan's recent extended absence due to his illness. Elspeth wasn't disappointed, herself. Honeymoons were about the sort of intimate discovery of each other that was a little frightening to contemplate when you were marrying a man you had seen five times, had had four letters and three phone calls from and kissed once.

Cousin Amanda's reaction was echoed by all Elspeth's friends, however, not to mention Mr and Mrs Moore, and even Elspeth's brother Rodney, who was following in his father's footsteps in the firm of Glynn, Moore, Banks and Morton.

'So you mean,' he said, 'that we all spend the night in Darwin, you get dressed up, we fly to Borra-whatsit——'

'Gidgee,' she corrected patiently.

'—have the ceremony and then fly back to Darwin, leaving you to get out of your lace and put on your uniform?'

'Basically, yes,' she nodded calmly, 'although you're exaggerating about the uniform. I won't start work until Monday.'

'Oh, well, you always have been the odd one in the family. . .'

There was a wicked part of her that enjoyed her family's response. If she had thought she was really hurting them, it would have been different, but when she was only challenging their belief that there was only one way to have a wedding, and that was with eight bridesmaids, a live waltz-playing band, and two hundred and fifty guests, she thought they could take it.

The last Friday in May arrived, and the Moore family,

with wedding clothes carefully hung in zipped plastic
suit-bags, boarded their plane for Darwin, stepping out
into the dry, mild air of the town at five o'clock.

They checked in at Darwin's best hotel, and Elspeth
and her mother made a quick trip to the florist and
hairdresser to confirm arrangements for tomorrow morning. At half-past seven the family met Jane, who was to
be Elspeth's sole and singular bridesmaid, in the restaurant of the hotel, and an elegant, lengthy dinner
ensued.

Actually it was a lovely meal. Jane's presence meant
that no one wanted to bring up any of the small tensions
that could at times exist within the Moore family, and
Elspeth was reminded of how much she really did love
her family after all. It was simply that they were different
from herself, that was the thing, and it was neither their
fault nor hers.

She almost forgot the fact that she was getting married
tomorrow. . .until she climbed into bed in the single
room that adjoined her parents' room in the top-floor
suite. What did Lachlan look like? Friends in Melbourne
had demanded a photo and she didn't have one—again,
to their disappointment. Now she badly needed one, if
only to remind herself that his beard wasn't quite as
bushy as she was picturing it, and that his tan was more
healthy-looking. Those blue eyes, too. . .she knew they
were bright and twinkling and warm, but she couldn't
see them. She was marrying a stranger.

In the darkness of the night, her fears and uncertain-
ties began to grow. She barely slept, and in the morning
she found that she was seized with nausea.

Emerging from the bathroom after a wretched ten
minutes over the basin, she found her mother sitting on
the bed studying her accusingly. 'You're not pregnant,
are you? Is that why this wedding is so hasty?'

'No, of course I'm not!' Elspeth exclaimed, embarrassed and outraged.

'Hm, well. . .'

'I'm nervous. Isn't that what a bride is supposed to be?'

'Not in this day and age,' her mother answered. 'That was for girls who didn't know the facts of life.' Then she added a little bitterly, 'Of course, if you were getting married in front of two hundred and fifty people with a train and a veil to worry about, and video equipment, I could understand nerves, but out in the bush——'

'Mums,' interrupted Elspeth desperately. 'Do you mind leaving me by myself till it's time for the hairdresser?'

'What about breakfast, darling? You should try to——'

'I'll just have a tray in my room.'

'I'll order it then, love. What would you like?' Mrs Moore had thrown aside the careful well-modulated voice that Elspeth associated with charity dinners and was speaking in the ordinary, unaffected tones she remembered from her childhood.

'Anything,' she answered. 'Whatever you think looks best and most nourishing.'

'I'll be cross if you don't eat it. . .'

'I know. I will eat it, I promise.'

And she did: fruit salad, toast, coffee, scrambled eggs and bacon, although it cost her a good deal of effort and determination to do so. Two hours later, she stood in front of the full-length mirror with her mother and Jane hovering beside her.

'Your hair looks absolutely goregous, Ellie.'

'Yes, I must say she did a surprisingly good job,' Mum agreed, 'for a salon in this backwater. And the flowers are just right, too.'

Elspeth wore her chestnut-gold hair in a cascading

halo of soft, loose curls, framed on top by an arc of tiny apricot-pink rosebuds in a delicate fuzz of fern and baby's breath. She carried a matching bouquet, as did Jane, whose rustling taffeta dress was the same colour as the rosebuds only slightly darker.

'Well. . .' Mrs Moore said, taking a final critical look at her own Nile-green silk, 'Rodney and Charles are already downstairs, I imagine. It's time to go.'

It seemed odd to be travelling to one's own wedding in a light plane, and it added to the feeling Elspeth was increasingly aware of—that this wasn't her at all. Somehow, she had become trapped inside another person's body and another person's life, and she was the only one who had noticed.

Dad had said something to her in a quiet, serious voice as they crossed the breezy tarmac to the small, specially-chartered plane. 'It's not too late to change your mind. Don't go through with it because of what other people might say or feel if you don't. *After* the ceremony, that's when it's too late.' Elspeth nodded and felt a lump come into her throat suddenly. When Dad wasn't thinking about business he could be so kind. . . Then her dress whipped up in the wind and the moment was broken as she concentrated on keeping the wayward skirt in place.

Dad's words kept echoing in her mind as she stared down from the window, oblivious to the drone of the plane's engine, at the rich carpet of Walkadu National Park that crept past below them now. One part of her thrilled to the beauty of the paper-bark forests and park-like flatlands broken up by rust-red castles of rock and gorges that revealed secret pools and cascades as the plane flew over. The rest of her wondered about the meaning of her own feelings. Did she want to run away from this wedding? No, it wasn't that. It was more that she couldn't feel at home in the role of a bride, especially when the groom to whose life she would be joining hers was such a hazy figure. She did not feel dread, or even reluctance, only confusion.

The plane had passed beyond the huge national park and was flying over cattle country now. Great herds of the reddish beasts lumbered at a half-run away from the noise of the low-flying engine. The grass looked plentiful but dry. Borragidgee couldn't be much further. . . Yes, the descent was beginning. It didn't take long, and soon the landing gear was bumping gently along the hard, raised surface of the airstrip.

A man in clerical robes came to meet them, grinning in a relaxed way. He was going bald, but looked to be only in his early forties.

'I'm David Johnson,' he said, putting out a hand to each of them in turn. There was laughter as Elspeth juggled with her bouquet to free her right hand.

'The flying bishop?' she said.

'That's right. And your celebrant for today.' He led them towards the new-looking Toyota four-wheel drive that waited at the edge of the strip.

'An odd combination of roles—minister and chauffeur,' Mr Moore said.

'One way of ensuring that the bridal party isn't late,' the bishop quipped.

The drive was short and Elspeth, in the front seat next to her mother, was aware of Mrs Moore's frequent glances.

She wants to know how I'm reacting to Borragidgee, Elspeth realised, but in fact the tiny town was passing in a blur, and only the events ahead had any meaning or importance.

A small white church, set on stilts as so many buildings were in this part of the country, came into view as Bishop Johnson swung the car into an empty space of ground beside it. It looked neat and new, but oleander, wattle and bougainvillaea already grew up around the wooden lattice-work that enclosed the stilting. There seemed to be quite a crowd gathered in front of the church. The whole town appeared to be there. Elspeth was dimly aware of it as she negotiated the high step down from the Toyota, handing her bouquet to Jane, who gave her a quick, impulsive hug and whispered, 'This is going to be wonderful!'

Bishop Johnson hurried over to make the unnecessary announcement that the bridal party had arrived, Mr Moore stepped to Elspeth's side to take her arm ready for their walk into the church and down the aisle, and Mrs Moore came close to give her daughter a last kiss. The crowd by the church was thinning now as people disappeared inside, and some urchin children who were too restless to sit through the ceremony scampered barefoot around the side of the building to play.

'Oh, good! We can see the groom's party at last!' Mrs Moore exclaimed, studying the group from the distance of twenty yards at which she and the rest of the bridal party stood. 'Now which one. . .don't tell me! The tall one. . .that's not *him*, is it?'

CHAPTER THREE

ELSPETH looked. Two men in charcoal-grey suits stood waiting. One of them, of modest height, must be Peter Dane, the owner-manager of the nearest cattle station who was their best man. The other man. . . Ellie frowned.

'Nn—yes! That *is* Lachlan!' She almost hadn't recognised him. His hair had been cut so that it fell just below his collar at the back and he was clean-shaven. From this distance, his face took on a strong, firm appearance, but she could not see much more than that. His tan looked different too. Perhaps that was just because she was seeing him in the grey suit, not in the casual khaki, white or blue shirts he had worn on four of the five times they had seen each other.

'He doesn't look a bit like I imagined from what you described,' Camilla Moore said crossly. 'He's quite. . .' She didn't finish. 'They're waving. They must be waiting to take Rodney and me into the church. That's lovely of them.'

She and Rodney left, soon joining the two men with smiles and greetings. They all disappeared. Elspeth, Jane and Mr Moore were now the only ones left outside. Faintly they heard the wheezy but tuneful notes of an old organ starting up, a tune that would mark time for a few bars until the start of the wedding march that everyone recognised.

'That's our cue, I think,' her father said.

'I'm ready,' Elspeth answered breathlessly, clutching her bouquet more tightly.

Jane moved forward and Elspeth followed on her

father's arm. They arrived at the door just as the organ burst forth into the traditional melody. The aisle of the plainly lit church, with its pews of pale wood was not long and soon Elspeth had arrived at Lachlan's side. Their eyes met and he smiled at her, his teeth white and even in his tanned face. It was a smile that gave her a solid, relief-filled confidence, even while she was confusedly wondering just what it was that made him look so different now.

No time to think about this. The ceremony passed in a whirl. Elspeth listened to Lachlan's deep-voiced responses and gave her own, felt his warmth at her side and then his fingers gently guiding the plain gold band on to her finger, heard the singing and found that her own usually strong alto voice would only come out as a thin thread. The bishop gave his final pronouncement, Lachlan's lips touched hers gently for a moment, they put their names to the clean page of the parish register, and then it was over. It was done. It was irrevocable.

'There's always divorce,' Lachlan had said, but divorce was not a going back to what had been before, and, overwhelmed by the solemnity of the words she had just spoken, Elspeth made her own private vow that she would make everything of this if she possibly could.

Now they were out in the sunshine again and her mother was kissing Lachlan. 'I hadn't imagined someone quite so. . .well, so *imposing*,' she said with a little laugh, one that Elspeth recognised as the laugh Mrs Moore used when she felt she was expected to flirt mildly with her husband's business friends.

Lachlan only grinned ruefully. 'Imposing? Is that what I am? Oh, dear!'

'Oh, I meant it as a compliment.'

'Yes, I know you did,' he answered seriously this time. 'Thank you.'

Ellie was thinking, Imposing? Is that what it is that I

never noticed in Darwin? Impulsively she turned to him, taking advantage of a lull between all the greetings and hugs and congratulations she had been receiving from strangers whose faces she had not yet even begun to absorb over the last five minutes. 'Lachlan, what was the illness that sent you to Darwin? You never said. . .'

'Illnesses,' he corrected with a smile, not questioning her odd remark at such a time. He had a large, comforting hand in hers. 'A gastric complaint followed by a bad bout of malaria, and then hepatitis A, all one on top of the other. Unfortunately I was idiotic enough to try and push through all three. I collapsed once the hepatitis hit, and of course I was infectious so I had to steer clear of any work then.'

'Odd thing to be talking about just now,' Peter Dane said, 'when I haven't even been properly introduced to the bride.'

A round of more formal introductions began—the people from the cattle station, the schoolteacher Jim Partridge, the three Aboriginal health workers Florence, Annie and Leonie, and the elders of the local Aboriginal community, as well as a couple of people, including a rather cool-looking woman in large, dark-rimmed sunglasses, that Ellie couldn't categorise or place at all. Lachlan seemed to sense her bewilderment.

'Don't worry,' he said. 'I'll explain everyone for you later, and it'll soon fall into place.' The crowd thinned and two four-wheel-drive vehicles headed off down the dusty main street. 'The Danes are going back out to Nagadi to do some last-minute things towards the meal,' Lachlan said. Nagadi was the cattle station, and the Dane family had generously offered their homestead as a venue for the low-key wedding reception. 'Perhaps your family would like to have a look at the house and the medical centre, then we'll head out that way too.'

Elspeth nodded and felt his arm tighten around her

shoulders in a strong squeeze. The thin, bearded man with the yellowish tan that she remembered from Darwin had gone, and his place seemed to have been taken by a strongly built stranger with a healthy outdoor complexion and a cleanly squared jaw, who was comfortable and at home in this, to her own senses, alien environment. He couldn't know how this was turning her feelings upside down, nor how each reassurance he gave her only added to her sense of dislocation: she hadn't married a slightly shy, slightly awkward man who was taking as tentative a step into the future as she was herself; she had married a man who seemed completely the master of his own destiny, and now of hers too.

But the medical centre and house, she found, belonged to both the Lachlans she was beginning to know. The Moores listened and looked politely as he showed them over the small but efficient medical centre. Jane showed the interest of a fellow professional, and Elspeth took in each feature with the knowledge that it would all become as familiar to her over the coming months as the back of her own hand. Lachlan's explanation of the facilities, including the two-way radio and tiny three-bed ward, was confident and professional. Clearly he felt a pride in the place, which contained several of his own innovations.

Once he had shown them into the residential part of the building, however, he became more like the quieter man she had known in Darwin.

'Well,' he said, taking in the various rooms with a sweeping gesture. 'It's self-explanatory, isn't it? That room there——' he pointed to an open door '—is, well, I apologise for it. I've started collecting a few things over the past couple of years. Tried to sort them out last week, but didn't get far. Perhaps I'll close the door.'

He glanced at Ellie as he did so and she realised that, beneath the change in his manner, he was anxious about her reaction to the house. For a moment she couldn't even work out why, then the answer came, utterly obvious. She would be living here. This was her home. It was not that she had forgotten this, of course, but somehow she had been far more interested in Lachlan's mood than in the colours of the curtains and the state of the light fittings.

She smiled at him and saw the quick relief in his answering grin. His blue eyes twinkled in an expression that was meant only for her. He *had* been worried. His next words came briskly again. 'It's too new to have a lot of character yet, of course, but it's bright and cool, and the stained wood beams are nice I think. The enclosed veranda too. The garden should start to look more impressive soon.'

He led them out through the front door and Elspeth was left with only a confused awareness of cream-painted walls, dark ceiling beams, boldly patterned curtains in the lounge-room and muted textured ones elsewhere and, in the bedroom, a large double bed covered with a beautiful hand-made patchwork quilt in a varied assortment of reds and blues.

After a short tour of the fledgling garden, they all piled into the Toyota and began the drive out to Nagadi. The town, with its dusty main street, school, church, untidy general store and scattering of small dwellings, was soon left behind, and they were driving through grassland, sparsely wooded with eucalyptus and studded with hard, sturdy termite mounds that frequently rose to a height of six feet or more. It was harsh country, subject to fire, flood and drought—perpetual and unpredictable reminders that human beings would never fully tame this land—but it had a rugged, proud beauty, both in its flat lands and in the suddenly encountered gash of a gorge through the terrain or the worn outcropping of red or brown-gold rock.

It was about twenty miles out to Nagadi, a tiny distance by outback standards. Elspeth was beside Lachlan in the front seat, with her mother by the window at her left. It was rather cramped and Camilla Moore had fussed a little, as they had climbed in, about the possibility of their dresses getting crumpled. Clearly she was not expecting too much luxury at the Nagadi homestead.

Lachlan pointed out a flock of cockatoos and an unusually large termite mound, but the drive passed largely in silence, allowing Elspeth to become very aware of the man—her husband!—beside her. 'Imposing'. Mrs Moore's archly-spoken label came back to her. The word could have been 'attractive'. There had certainly been an assessment made of his looks, and Camilla Moore had exaggerated the way she had to look up at him as if naughty Elspeth had never mentioned that he was so magnificently *tall*.

It came as a bit of a shock suddenly to realise that she had married a good-looking man, and for the first time Ellie wondered if there were any quietly bruised or broken hearts in the Borragidee region as the result of their marriage. . .wondered, too, why he hadn't married long before this. Most men of his age would have some kind of past. 'There's always divorce.' Again the words came back to her, and with a shock of doubt she wondered suddenly if he had been married before. It was awful to think that she didn't have a clue.

'This is Nagadi.' It was Lachlan speaking. 'The homestead should come into view any minute. . . Yes, there.'

The stilted building rose from among a scattered group of outbuildings, a comfortable old place with wide verandas on three sides that were shaded by a long slope of dark green galvanised iron roof. Two rows of small paper lanterns were strung all the way around the veranda, looped between each pillar, and big potted palms edged a strip of Persian-patterned carpet that ran from the front door to the bottom of the steps to form a special entry for the bride and groom.

The area was soon crowded with guests clapping and cheering, and as she came through the door and into the cool dimness of the lounge-room Elspeth was almost blinded by the repeated click of a very professional camera's flash-bulb. The photographer lowered the camera as the bridal couple brushed past and Ellie saw that it was the cool-looking woman she had met outside the church—what was her name? Something that matched her cool, crisp façade. Jacqueline Harcourt, that was right.

She was looking faintly, cynically amused and faintly, cynically bored, and the camera that was suspended round her neck with a black leather strap gave her the air of a professional photographer who had attended far too many weddings before. She couldn't *be* a professional photographer, of course, and once again Elspeth wondered how she fitted into the Borragidgee scene.

'Forgive me for saying this, but I'm already very curious about how you're going to fit in.' It was Jacqueline herself using the words not five minutes later, and Elspeth started guiltily, spilling a fizzy puddle of champagne on to her capable nurse's hand. Someone had just thrust the glass at her and it was very full. One too-generous sip had already sent bubbles fizzing up her nose.

Jacqueline gave a pitying glance. 'Got a napkin?'

'No. . . I'll just. . .' Ellie transferred the glass to her left hand and, still feeling thoroughly like a nurse caught out by climsiness while on duty, was just about to wipe the pale froth of liquid on the front of her dress as if it was a surgical gown. Coming to the horrified realisation that in fact this was her wedding dress, she caught herself in time and accepted Jacqueline Harcourt's ministering gesture with a paper serviette.

The awkward moment didn't improve her balance of confidence with this woman who, she now realised, was English, and very sophisticated English at that.

'Do you like what you've seen of the place so far?' Jacqueline went on, once order had been restored.

'Well, I haven't really seen anything,' Ellie answered.

'First impressions, I'm talking about. The church? The main street? The drive here? The homestead? There's not a lot else, you know. Nothing that you'll be seeing on a daily basis, anyway. If you get any time off. . .'

'I'm afraid the wedding took up all my. . . I don't think I had any first impressions.'

'On second thoughts, perhaps that's just as well,' Jacqueline drawled.

'What do you mean?'

'Well, frankly, Borragidgee's the end of the earth. I'm sure you knew that in theory. . .'

'Actually, I——'

'. . .but seeing it in the flesh, so to speak, I wondered if you were suffering from shell-shock.'

'If you think it's such an awful place,' Elspeth retorted coldly, 'I wonder what *you're* doing living here.'

There was something very irritating in the woman's attitude. She was looking at Elspeth as if the latter was some new and potentially rather amusing species of creature to be studied, and as if the wedding outfit which other people had been so nice about was merely an eccentric and ridiculous plumage.

'Me?' Jacqueline was saying, 'Oh, haven't you been told? I'm only living here temporarily. A couple more months. I'm a journalist. . .a *writer*,' she amended quickly, as if it sounded much better that way. 'And I'm doing a book on the place. With photos.' She flourished her camera.

'There must be something interesting about it then,' Ellie pointed out lightly, 'or it'll be a very short book.'

The mild irony brought a tinkling laugh from the English journalist. 'Well, of course there is *politically*,' she said. 'The ongoing oppression of the Aboriginal people, the wholesale destruction of the environment, the uranium question, the inter-relationship between the different interest groups. It'll sell incredibly well in the current climate of thinking. This is frontier territory for all those issues—which are so-o-o complex—and a journalist has to be there in depth to capture the truth.'

'Of course,' Ellie murmured.

If the issues were so complex, she was thinking, could they be analysed properly by someone who lived here for just a few months and who didn't even like the place? Instinctively Elspeth thought she would have much more confidence in what Lachlan had to say about the situation.

Lachlan. Her husband. He was here at her side suddenly, greeting her with a touch of his arm around her waist. Greeting Jacqueline Harcourt too, and with surprising warmth.

'Hello, Jackie! I haven't really caught up with you yet today. How are things going?'

'They couldn't be better,' she replied keenly. 'I had a fabulous trip out to Walgunya last week and stayed overnight. Peter Dane took me. It was absolutely mind-boggling to see what's being achieved there. I spent the rest of the week glued to my typewriter.'

'Walgunya is a cattle station being run completely by Aboriginal people now,' Lachlan explained quickly to Elspeth, then he turned back to Jackie's flow of enthusiastic words.

Elspeth soon gathered a little cynically that much of

the enthusiasm came from the journalist's vanity having been thoroughly satisifed during her two-day tour. A feast had been prepared specially for her, followed by a corroboree in her honour, and she had been shown a scared site that apparently no white woman had ever been allowed to see before, due to an amazing rapport she had intuitively found with one of the older women on the property.

Lachlan nodded energetically and seemed fasincated and approving of the whole thing. Elspeth was surprised. She hadn't expected him to be so warm towards this woman who used the pronouns 'I' and 'me' at least twice in every sentence. Wasn't he at all sceptical about her sincerity?

Or is it just me being catty, Elspeth wondered uncomfortably, because she hasn't given us any congratulations. . .? And because she's a very attractive woman, a more dangerous voice added in the depths of her mind.

Jacqueline Harcourt *was* attractive, undeniably so. She wore her bleached blonde hair very short so that it stood up aggressively on her perfectly shaped head and attained a casual mussed up look when she ran her long slim fingers through it as she talked. The bone-structure of her face was classically faultless, which was what allowed her to get away with such a businesslike hairstyle and yet still appear utterly feminine.

Her lips were glossed in a bold pink and her blue eyes—nearly the same astonishing blue as Lachlan's— were made large and glowing by the skilful blend of silver-white tones of shadow beneath surprisingly dark, arched brows, fashionably unplucked. Her skin glowed, too, with both natural tan and an almost translucent make-up which was definitely more expensive than anything Elspeth had ever tried. Certainly, though, she would look just as good without any make-up at all since she had the lazy, inborn attributes of beauty that made

Ellie feel so clumsy and flawed by contrast, and seemed to make a mockery of her frowning sessions in front of the mirror.

Elspeth felt her bridal glow beginning to ebb under this reluctant onslaught of resentment against Jacqueline. It seemed petty to be feeling this way, and she shook it off by detaching herself from Lachlan's side—he barely noticed, apparently—and going in search of an hors d'oeuvre or two from the big platters that were now being passed around the room. Taking a mushroom vol-au-vent and a shrimp canapé, she went out on to the veranda where at least half of the milling guests had spilled.

Camilla Moore caught her daughter's eye and beckoned her over. 'Coping, darling?' She brushed a wayward chestnut curl back over her daughter's shoulder.

'Yes, of course, why shouldn't I be?' Ellie answered a little touchily, aware that she *hadn't* coped too well with Jacqueline Harcourt.

'Well, because you're the bride! The centre of attention! And you've never enjoyed being that,' her mother elaborated.

'I'm not sure that I am, though—the centre of attention, I mean.' Before she could stop herself, Ellie had glanced back towards the doorway to catch sight of Lachlan stepping on to the veranda, closely followed by Jacqueline. She held a bottle of champagne and was filling his glass to the brim, laughing off his protests as mere artificial politeness on his part, which no doubt they were.

Mrs Moore caught her daughter's frown and saw the direction of her gaze. 'Oh, darling! Don't tell me that you're not sure of him. . .sure of his love?'

'Yes, of course I am.' It was another hollow assurance. How could she tell her mother that she wasn't sure of anything in this marriage, least of all her own feelings?

Love had never been mentioned. A practical, sensible arrangement. What on earth did that mean?

But her mother was still talking. 'Don't endanger your life together with jealousy at this stage,' Camilla Moore was saying. 'Not at any stage. I've seen it destroy three of my friends' marriages. She's leaving in a few months, isn't she? And he married you, not her.'

It was intended as reassurance, but it had the opposite effect. If Mums had noticed the way Jackie Harcourt was monopolising Lachlan without protest from him, then it wasn't just Elspeth's own imagination. . .

'Buffet's on,' said Rodney, coming up to them with a heavily piled plate of meats and salads. 'Better hurry and line up because I'm not sure there's enough.'

Elspeth and Mrs Moore followed his gesturing arm obediently but without alarm. Rodney always thought that there wouldn't be enough, wrongly judging all appetites to be as hearty as his own. 'Time's going by, too. Pilot says we'll have to leave here within half an hour if we're to get back to Darwin tonight.'

This was taken more seriously and drew an emotional wail from Mrs Moore. 'Will you be all right, Ellie? Should we try to stay the night, to be *with* you?'

Rodney gave a shout of laughter. 'Stay the night? That'd be the last thing in the world Ellie'd want. Not to mention poor Lachlan. Wedding night! Honestly, Mum!'

Elspeth blushed and Mrs Moore tripped over her words. 'I don't mean. . . Don't be silly, Rodney! There's no need for that kind of—I only meant perhaps we could arrange to stay the night here at the homestead so we could see Ellie through to the end of the evening.'

'Sorry, I misunderstood.' Rodney grinned unrepentantly, biting at a large king prawn that must have been flown in from Darwin specially for tonight's feast, perhaps in the cargo hold of their own chartered plane. He went off to find Mr Moore and Jane to hurry them through the meal as well.

Leaving in half an hour. It began to sink in. Then Ellie would be alone in this crowd of people with no one but Lachlan to support her, and where was Lachlan now? She began to look for him almost frantically as she stood in the press of strangers, at least half of whom she hadn't been introduced to yet, who were reaching over the big buffet table and filling their plates. Where was he? Still with Jacqueline?

She twisted and turned to take in the whole room. Faces smiled at her. They all knew who she was and were eager to welcome her and give her their blessings and congratulations. Some of them might have come from a hundred miles away for this event, but she couldn't give out response after response to all their warm wishes. Faces, voices and identities were rapidly becoming a blur.

At last, just in time to damp down a rising sense of panic, Lachlan caught her eye above the crowd and was pushing his way towards her.

'I thought I'd lost you,' he said, and pulled Ellie against him, pressing his firm lips to her forehead and holding his long arm around her waist. 'Jackie's hard to get away from sometimes. She's. . . I don't know,' he finished with a shrug and an absent frown, as if the English journalist was a problem that preoccupied him and irked him more than he would have liked.

'What is she?' Elspeth probed lightly, needing to know more about what he really thought and felt. His words didn't jell with the animated response he had given Jackie.

'Not our concern tonight, anyway,' he finished, unsatisfactorily.

He kept her with him after this, all through the meal, which was interrupted midway through the buffet course by the cutting of the cake. It was an oddly timed ritual, performed quickly so that Elspeth's family could see it before they had to leave to make their flight, but the guests, accustomed to the topsy-turvy ways of the outback, rallied round with an enthusiastic sense of occasion so that it wasn't a disappointing moment.

The cake, flown from Darwin along with the seafood, was rich and fruity, and the knife plunged into it with a smooth movement. Elspeth could not take the credit for this. It was Lachlan's hand, warm and smooth as it lay over her own slightly freckled one, that provided most of the pressure. She was too aware of him to think about using her own strength. He stood behind her, his torso shielding her and moulding itself to her own in the same way that his palm moulded itself to the back of her hand, and his free arm came under her breast and across her stomach in a gesture of support and protection.

She felt the newly clean lines of his jaw and cheek as he rubbed them gently against her richly highlighted hair and had a sudden longing to abandon the cake and the sight of the eager onlookers and turn in to his arms to feel the soft crush of her breasts against his hard chest and the lean lines of his thighs against hers.

Then as they pulled the knife, sticky with a sweet, spicy smear of fruit, from the heart of the rich cake she had a different awareness—not physical but emotional, a sudden understanding of the symbolic nature of this first joint action of their married life. They were together, a unified force in everything they did. Even a humble action like using a knife to cut cake could be shared, could be proportioned out between their different strengths. Would they manage to carry this symbol through to their everyday lives as they were supposed to? Or would the love that was missing in their relationship have the same effect as missing out eggs from a fruit cake, creating a crumbling structure that refused to bind together?

It was a question she didn't know how to answer, and had no more time to think about as the awkward and emotional moment of farewelling her family and Jane came swiftly upon her. The charter pilot was jiggling one leg impatiently and Peter Dane, who was to drive them back to the airstrip at Borragidgee, was insisting seriously that they really must hurry. Only emergency take-offs were permitted from the strip after dark, and sunset was fast approaching. Mrs Moore was in tears. . . Mr Moore was talking gruffly about Melbourne being only half a day away by plane. . . Rodney made a teasing comment. The four-wheel-drive started up and everyone piled in. From the window Jane gave a grin and a wave that contained a hint of wistful envy, and then they were gone.

The lull in the atmosphere lasted only a moment, then talk and laughter broke out again as loud as ever. Hot dishes were being brought to the buffet now—a steaming pile of savoury rice, an enormous chicken casserole, pasta with a rich tomato-filled sauce, and several other things. The rest of the cake—minus the pieces the Moores had been given—was taken away to the kitchen to be cut up for the other guests later on. Everyone told Elspeth in a confused gabble how lovely her family was, how she would miss them, but how so much would be done to make her feel at home here. . . It got dark, and the remnants of the lavish meal were cleared away. Lachlan, who had fielded many of the questions and comments addressed to Elspeth, said quietly to her, 'Want to go for a walk outside? I'm sick of being the chief attraction, aren't you?'

She nodded. 'If you think they'll all forgive us. . .'

'They will. One more short appearance while they

parcel out the cake, and then we can go. . .if they've left our car alone.'

'They wouldn't do anything too dramatic, would they?' Elspeth asked anxiously, thinking of friends in Melbourne who had had sugar poured in their petrol tank by a too-lively crowd of bachelor mates.

'Not when it's the doctor's official vehicle,' he assured her.

This talk had brought them to the edge of the veranda and down the steps. It had been getting hot inside the spacious homestead, Ellie now realised, with all the people pressed inside. Out here, the earth had already thrown much of the day's warmth back into the star-crusted depths of the outback sky, and it was refreshingly cool to walk among the gnarled old peppertrees that mingled with native eucalyptus and acacia to form a tangy-scented park-like expanse.

'Happy with the day, Ellie?' Lachlan asked softly, breaking a silence that had fallen when they reached the trees. His arm was around her and tentatively she returned his gesture. Among the crowd of unfamiliar guests his touch had been a reassurance, but now that they were alone it was a reminder of the fact that much of their life together and their discovery of each other would take place behind closed doors, just the two of them, and that that process would begin tonight. How would she respond to the full intimacy of his touch when their bodies pressed nakedly together?

'Yes, very happy with it.' Her answer had come after a pause and a long inward breath, and she stiffened as she realised that he had noticed her preoccupation with other thoughts. With a tighter squeezing around her waist he stopped her, and they stood facing each other beneath the trailing branches of a peppertree while he searched her eyes, lifting her chin with a gentle touch of his fingers beneath her jaw.

'Happy with it so far,' he said. 'But it's later tonight, isn't it? When we get home?'

'Yes, I. . . Silly!' Pointless to deny it, but hard to make the admission.

'I suppose this is old-fashioned,' he said. 'So many couples. . .most couples. . .must have already taken that step, but our situation is different.'

She nodded breathlessly. 'When love. . .isn't at the centre of it, when we've had other more practical reasons——'

'Love?' He echoed the word in an odd tone, interrupting her groping phrases. 'Yes, we decided not to talk about that, didn't we? We talked about all sorts of other things.'

'Actually, after the night of the accident, we didn't talk much at all. We couldn't. We didn't see each other.'

'Do I seem unfamiliar? Is that part of it?' His hands rested lightly on her shoulders, but he was holding himself back somehow.

'Yes.' She seized on his suggestion with relief. Their three week separation. Of course that would add to her feeling of strangeness. 'You even look different, now that your illness has past. The beard, your tan, and you've put on weight. You were so thin before. . .' She was running on, and trailed off as she realised this.

'You preferred the old me?' He smiled, just a play at the corner of his lips.

'No, I don't think so. . .'

'Perhaps the only way to get over this. . .whatever it is. . .is to. . .'

He didn't finish. Ellie found that her gaze was almost mesmerised into locking with his as he pulled her to him and then her lids slid shut as her eyes began to swim and she was lost in a world of blind, wonderful sensation. His lips didn't touch hers at first but pressed to her cheeks, her throat, the hollows between her neck and shoulders, sending shivers of pleasure and awareness radiating over her body like ripples on a pond.

When he did find her mouth her own lips were already softly parted and waiting, eager to discover the taste and texture of him. His body began to mould itself to her own and his hands caressed the long curves of her back and thighs, making the silk of her under-dress wash with a slight rustle against her tingling skin. Her own fingers demanded to know the feel of him and when she slipped her hand up beneath his white shirt and massaged the firm muscles of his back, the low groan that sounded deep in his chest was not one of protest.

They had kissed once before, but this was different. Then, the first time, it had come out of emotional shock and the need for physical reassurance. Now it came from the early embers of respectful tenderness and an awareness of their sealed and official partnership. Oddly Victorian, and yet with nothing chaste or prim in the way they were beginning to discover each other.

Ellie slid her hands round to find his chest, pulling away from him a little without losing the ecstasy of his mouth. His skin was as soft as her own but textured roughly with curling hair that delighted her sensitive fingers with its contrast. He became impatient with the distance between their bodies and pulled her close again, plunging her body into warmth and complete sensation with a suddenness that made her gasp with delight. She had never felt this mingling of body-stirring newness and heart-warming familiarity before.

After a timeless, swirling exploration that could have lasted minutes or an hour, she felt his intensity slacken and, with both of them breathless and half-numb, he released her, then cradled her against his shoulder gently. She heard the low vibration of his voice against her ear as it came deep from his chest. 'Perhaps we don't have anything to worry about after all.'

'No, I don't think we do,' she managed to reply.

Slowly, still entwined together, they made their way back to the house.

'Ready for the cake?' It was Peter Dane, his stocky figure greeting them as they came across the veranda and into the house. 'We got it all cut up about half an hour ago and people have coffee and liqueurs but then. . .well, we couldn't find you and. . .'

'You didn't want to look too hard?' Lachlan finished with a wry drawl.

'Er. . .exactly.' He shifted awkwardly, a bachelor himself, then grinned. 'But not to worry. No one's been bored and you're here now.'

Elspeth was plunged once again into the confusing sea of faces and voices as the cake was parcelled out. Someone gave her coffee and she had to refuse a liqueur because she didn't have any spare hands, until the cool voice of Jacqueline Harcourt suggested that she take a seat someone had just vacated for her beside a small coffee-table. 'Then you can put your liqueur glass down there.'

The English journalist had picked up a brimming glass of thick amber liquid from the tray held by Peter Dane's younger brother and had ushered Elspeth into the chair before she could protest that actually she didn't really want a liqueur.

When Ellie was safely seated Jacqueline sat down beside her. 'You seem a bit bridal all of a sudden,' she said.

'Bridal?'

'Yes, you know. . .blushing, flustered.'

'Oh—well, I'm not. Just tired.'

'Is that what it is?' Jackie shrugged and looked sceptical. 'There's a thread pulling loose in your lace.'

'Is there? Oh, dear!!' Ellie looked down at her front in the direction of Jackie's gaze and saw that it was true.

The spidery lace of the bodice was gathered and pulled in one spot where a loop of thread had pulled out. It must have happened outside, and it seemed from Jackie's manner that she, like Peter Dane only with a different attitude, was well aware of the time Elspeth and Lachlan had spent beneath the peppertree.

Elspeth felt anger rising. English people were supposed to be reserved about such things and to have a respect for the privacy of others. She didn't want suggestive comments from the blonde journalist, and had certainly not invited them. She didn't really want Jacqueline Harcourt sitting next to her at all.

But Jacqueline didn't go away. . .and where was Lachlan? She caught a glimpse of him in the adjoining dining-room, barely visible in the crush of people. It seemed that the outback dwellers took full advantage of a party when it was offered, and no one had any intention of going home yet.

'You seem a bit lost when Lachlan's not with you,' Jackie observed, as if curious about the subject.

'Do I?' It was an ineffectual parry, and the other woman ignored it.

'Actually,' she ploughed on immediately, 'from what Lachlan's told me about the reasons for this marriage, you're not a bit what I expected—if I can be blunt.'

'Would you be less blunt if I asked you to be?' Elspeth asked lightly, and the blonde journalist laughed a little too heartily, showing her pink gums for a moment.

'Probably not. I can't seem to help it, can I? My ruthless professional instincts, I suppose.' Clearly it was something she was quite proud of. 'No, I *am* curious about this,' she went on, 'Because it could fit into part of my book. The outback mentality. The two of you ready to contract marriage just for Lachlan's convenience. He gets a nurse with no accommodation hassles and an automatic residency permit. It took months for

me to get mine, and it's only temporary. But you. . .
I'm wondering now what you want to get out of it.'

Why should these words upset her so much? Ellie
wondered as she managed a token response and got
herself away to the safety of the pink-tiled bathroom at
the back of the homestead. It was only what Lachlan
had said himself, after all. Was it the fact that he hadn't
bothered to pretend to Jackie that there was any question
of love? Or was it that the journalist's direct phrasing
stripped away any illusion that a marriage of convenience
could also contain comfort, warmth and respect as well?
Perhaps it was the idea of herself and Lachlan meriting
an anecdotal paragraph in Jackie's racy book as a typical
example of an odd outback arrangement.

No, it was the naked coldness of it, the implication
that if he'd happened to get talking to a different nurse
in Darwin—Jane, say, or Rebecca or Sue—it might be
one of them who was now standing here miserably out
of place in a silk and lace dress.

Lachlan's not like that, one inner voice said to her.
How would I know? another part of herself answered.
Jackie's obviously known him for longer and knows him
better than I do.

The English journalist's face had fallen in astonishment as Elspeth made her trembling getaway. She had
seemed genuinely surprised at the realisation that her
words had hurt. Did the whole town think of the new
Mrs McLintock as simply a well-qualified nurse with a
marriage certificate attached?

Miserably, Elspeth splashed her hot face with some
cool water from the stiff brass tap above the basin, found
a clean hand-towel and patted herself dry. She couldn't
stay in here. Lachlan had said that they would leave once
they'd sat out the eating of the cake. He had implied
that he wanted to get away so that they could be alone.
She had lost faith in that now, but she wanted to get

away none the less, if only to hurry this day towards the peaceful conclusion of sleep.

Sleep. . . Ellie rolled over among pale tangled sheets and looked at the green glow of the small electric alarm-clock. It read 04.15. She must have slept, then, although it didn't feel like it. She struggled to become aware of what was going on. Something was wrong. Then it came to her: Lachlan was no longer beside her. The realisation tore her with a painful blend of relief and loss.

On the way home—yes, it *was* her home now—he had known that something was wrong, but Ellie's attempt to hide it had seemed to put him off enough so that he asked no questions. In fact, they were very silent as they drove, a silence that could almost have been that of a happily married couple relieved at getting some peace and quiet after a hectic evening.

Then had come their lovemaking. She had been rigid at first when he had slowly begun to undress her, and she had teetered on the edge of a tirade of words about what Jackie had said. No, the *way* she had said it, the coldness and cynicism of it. But how could she confront Lachlan with such a nebulous thing? He hadn't deceived her. What was her complaint? Then gradually, the painful buzz of thoughts like angry bees in her mind had begun to lose their focus as a stronger awareness took over, an awareness that was only concerned with here and with now. Her body was all that mattered, not the future or the past.

In the pale moonlight that reflected into the room, Ellie's dress and lacy, silky underclothing slipped to the floor with little rustling sighs like living things, brushing at her skin as they dropped and leaving her at first intensely vulnerable. But then his hot body, strong and apparently at ease in its nakedness, had enclosed hers and guided her to the bed, pulling her down on to the softness of cool linen sheets and caressing her rhythmically. She was aware of her femaleness as she had never been before, and when his lips began to explore the tender skin of her tingling breasts she lost her place in the universe so that there was nothing but their two selves and the magic and mystery of their climax together.

After it was over he did not let her go, and the urgency of their passionate discovery lulled seamlessly into the quiet tenderness of lazy cradling. He whispered her name, a flutter against her ear, and she felt him relax. The fingers that had been tracing lazy circles over her rounded hip and smooth thigh slackened in one last silvery trail on her skin, his breathing fell into a deep rhythmic pattern, and then she knew he was asleep.

For herself, sleep seemed hours away—perhaps because she wished so keenly that she *would* sleep. It seemed that if she did, she would be able to regain that state of warm, dark oblivion where she no longer wondered why she was here—or even who she was. The fact that Lachlan lay asleep with his tanned body curved to fit against hers like two spoons in a drawer seemed to make a question-mark out of her very identity.

A sick wave of reaction and anti-climax washed over her after the physical pinnacle of lovemaking they had so recently attained. What did that pinnacle mean except that, in some dark animal way which had nothing to do with love, they were compatible? They had both been wrong. This was no way to enter a marriage at all. They had taken the step, and it was a mistake.

And so, without her realising it, these unhappy thoughts had gradually clouded into disturbing dreams and finally a heavy sleep. . .

A dark shape loomed beside the bed, and it was Lachlan, fully dressed and peering down at her with a frown. 'Ellie?'

'Hm?' Her voice came out cracked and groggy.

'I've been called out.'

'Out?' She couldn't make sense of it at first.

'Yes. You didn't hear the knocking at the door?'

'No.'

'I doubt I'll be back before dawn, and it may take much longer. It's an Aboriginal girl on the outskirts of town. She's gone into labour and there's a problem. She's only sixteen, and wasn't due for another three weeks. . .'

Elspeth struggled into a sitting position. Her body felt stiff and sore as if her skin had been chafed in parts by their lovemaking, although they had both been gentle. The bedclothes slipped to her waist, leaving her full breasts vulnerable as they swung gently and became still, tingling with the sudden chill of the air against their pink tips. Quickly she pulled a sheet up and pressed it against her collarbone with the flat of her hand.

Lachlan seemed unaware of the nervous movement. He reached out and touched a quick hand to her bare shoulder. 'I'm so sorry, Ellie. But you know how it is. I have to go and I can't waste time.'

'I know,' she managed.

He leant towards her to kiss her quickly on the lips, and she instinctively reached her arms around his neck to press her face against his more closely. Before she had time to question her need for his touch he had gone, and again she was left vulnerable and half-naked against the chill of the pre-dawn air.

Their wedding night. She sat there, numb, leaning against the pillows and bed-head, her tender skin growing gradually colder. Their wedding night: he had been called out and she was alone. Jacqueline Harcourt, if she found out about it, would want permission to include the amusing incident in her book.

CHAPTER FOUR

ELSPETH turned, and turned again in the wide bed. There was light streaming into the room and making a red glare against her closed lids. No matter which way she lay, it seemed too bright. From the mists of irritable half-sleep, she floated up into full consciousness.

Daylight! Bright, hot sun, and the clock now said eleven. She found that she had sprawled across the entire width of the double bed at a diagonal and wondered if Lachlan had crept in just after dawn to find himself shut out of the tangle of bedding. She listened, but the house seemed silent. Perhaps he was sitting in the dining-room over morning coffee and one of the city newspapers that were flown in every two weeks.

Hastily, feeling too alone, she showered and dressed. Her belongings had been freighted in from Darwin while she was in Melbourne, but Lachlan hadn't unpacked them—out of respect for her privacy, she realised with a touch of warmth—so that she had to rummage among the suitcases and cartons that were piled in her side of the wardrobe in order to find a pair of crisp cotton trousers in a warm khaki-beige and a neat round-necked blouse splashed with a floral pattern of khaki, white and red.

Brushing out the fallen curling mass of her chestnut hair and scooping it up on each side with patterned tortoiseshell combs, then slipping her feet into tan sandals, Elspeth hurried down to the other end of the house, not wanting him to come and investigate the noise she had been making with the boxes.

She need not have worried, she realised, as she swung

66

almost breathlessly around the open door and into the kitchen, through which she could see the dining-room beyond. Lachlan wasn't here. The house remained silent and she was alone. Very alone, it suddenly seemed, as she stood in the middle of the kitchen floor listening to the hum of the fridge. Mechanically she began to prepare breakfast, finding orange-juice, cereal, milk, bread and coffee in sensible, well-ordered places. Lachlan was tidy but not finicky, she decided. There was one cupboard in which plastic containers and glass jars were piled in precarious confusion. It was tempting to look further at the contents of his kitchen—*their* kitchen, she reminded herself uneasily—but that smacked somehow of sneakiness, as if she was trying to find out more about the man she had married in underhand ways.

I'm not Jacqueline Harcourt, Elspeth reminded herself. I'm not looking for an in-depth interview.

Instead, once she had prepared breakfast, she took a detective novel from the temptingly full bookshelf in the lounge and began to read, knowing that she needed a distraction against listening constantly for Lachlan's return. Insistently the thought came to her that she should have gone with him, if only to quieten her own fears about what might be going on.

Should she try to find him after breakfast? But no, what if there was another call or a radio message from the Royal Flying Doctor Service? Helplessly she realised that she had no idea how the radio equipment worked. Had Lachlan taken a paging device with him? How on earth had he managed out here all alone until now? No wonder he had felt an urgent need for—for what? A nurse, an assistant, a companion. Not a loving wife.

Again she was awash with confusion about the surprise of their strong response to each other last night. She felt her body loosening and tingling again at the memory and wanted to shake off the feeling. If it hadn't been for last night's lovemaking, perhaps the thing would make sense. All those words she had said to herself over the preceding weeks—respect, trust, honour. Sensual rapture and delight, shared climax, fiery awareness even in memory; none of that had been anticipated at all.

She remembered that smug decision she had made the night they first met—that physically he wasn't her type. Picturing now his tall tanned frame, the square line of his jaw, his piercing blue eyes and the lean length of his sensitive fingers. . .other more intimate pictures, too. . .it was as if the man in the Rock Bar in Darwin was someone else.

She stood up angrily and cleared away her breakfast things with an abrupt clatter of crockery, then wiped the walnut stain of the table with an impatient gesture of the yellow dishcloth she had found beneath the sink. Clearly what she should be doing this morning—or this afternoon, since it was already past noon—was unpacking her things and putting them in some order instead of worrying pointlessly about Lachlan and about her new responsibilities as Borragidgee's nurse. If there had been important things for her to know, Lachlan would have told her about them.

It was a pleasure and a release to bump noisily around the bedroom with boxes and suitcases. Ellie found that he had left plenty of space for her belongings in drawers, wardrobe and cupboards, in his somewhat chaotic spare-room there was even an empty set of shelves where she could store books and favourite old ornaments and knick-knacks. Her self-conscious bustle masked the turmoil and confusion of her inner feelings and absorbed her to the extent that at two o'clock, when her task was half-done and Lachlan entered the room, she did not even hear him.

'Hello, Ellie.'

She whirled around, hot-cheeked, and a bundle of books thudded on to the carpeted floor. 'Lachlan. . .!'

'I was a long time. It couldn't be helped.'

'Of course not.'

'The baby was stillborn.' He gave a shuddering sigh and reached out for her, taking her in his arms, Elspeth knew at once, more for his own comfort than for her own.

He had a right to it. She just had time to see the haggard exhaustion and regret in his face, accentuated by the dark new growth of beard which he hadn't had a chance to shave off since yesterday morning.

'How. . .?' she began.

'It couldn't have been saved. There's no way I should reproach myself. . .but of course I do.'

He had pulled away from her and was pacing restlessly. One foot kicked at the scatter of books she had dropped, and absently he bent down and tidied them into a pile then balanced them on the bed, which she had made up neatly an hour ago. She saw the tension in the strong muscles of his shoulders and heard a crack in his knee joint as he made the abrupt movements.

'And the mother?' she asked as he was doing all this.

'I want her to come in for a couple of days but at the moment she's refusing. Physically she's come out of it well—surprisingly so; but mentally, emotionally, I'm not sure. I'm driving out to Nagadi to talk to one of our Aboriginal health workers, Florence Dixon. She was at the wedding yesterday. . .' He broke off and shook his head as if to get rid of a snarl of cobwebs.

'Yes, I met Florence.'

'Ellie, this is just the sort of beginning I didn't want for us.'

'Don't worry,' she said quickly. 'This is important.'

'It died *in utero* some days ago. She says she wasn't aware of a decrease in foetal movement. Father unknown. The girl—Nancy—has been in trouble for a couple of years now. She drifted off to Brisbane, came back two months ago heavily pregnant. No pre-natal care or counselling at all until we took a look at her, as far as I could make out. She'd been drinking and smoking heavily all through the pregnancy. Florence has had some success in getting her to cut back on that, but not a lot.'

'Let's go, shall we? Tell me about it as we drive,' Elspeth put in gently. She laid her fingers on his arm and he slid away then gripped her hand in his.

'You're coming out too?' His eyes seemed to focus on her property for the first time since he had entered the room.

'Of course. It's a twenty-mile drive, and you're exhausted.'

He nodded silently, took the keys from his back pocket and handed them to her. They left the house together, still without speaking, and he said nothing, too, when she slid in behind the wheel of the high four-wheel-drive and started the engine. It was the first time she had driven such a vehicle, but now was not the time to throw a fit of feminine helplessness.

She looked at the large gear-stick that rose beside her left knee and saw that it had the gear positions clearly marked on it. Handbrake? Yes, the kind that pulled out from under the dashboard. Lights, windscreen wipers, turning indicators—doubtful if she would need any of those on a bright afternoon in quiet Borragidgee. Carefully in neutral, Elspeth started the engine, depressed the clutch, put the vehicle into reverse and backed smoothly down the drive.

'You were telling me about Florence,' she finally said when they were safely on their way down the main street.

'Hm? Oh, yes. She's our best. Her father's a stockman out at Nagadi. Mother died several years ago and she has three little brothers to look after. Perhaps that's what makes her so good at her work. She's mature for her age, only twenty. She visits people, scolds and cajoles and lo! It often seems that they take more notice of her than they do of me.'

'But after all, that's the role of the Aboriginal health workers, isn't it?' Ellie questioned. His initial tightly strung exhaustion and self-blame seemed to be relaxing away a little now, and if talking helped as it seemed to. . .

'Yes, their actual training is pretty basic, but they can go into someone's place, give advice on hygiene and draw out background problems in a way that I never could, no matter how closely or strongly I was accepted in the community.'

'They. . .respect you, though?' Somehow she couldn't imagine otherwise, but he seemed to be denigrating his own status.

'Perhaps in one way they respect me too much. There are things they keep hidden from me because they're ashamed or they think I'll be angry. Florence is one of them, so they don't hide things from her nearly so much.'

'There are two other health workers here, aren't there?'

'Part-time, yes. Not as competent as Florence, but learning a lot from her. A bit inclined to go shy or giggly and forget to listen to instructions. I'm hoping that Florence will eventually go to Darwin and get full training as a nurse. At the moment she can't, of course, with her brothers all still at school, and perhaps it's just as well. By the time she's ready to go, Annie and Leonie will have settled down and be able to take over her role.'

'And you're hoping that Florence will——'

'Yes, persuade Nancy to come in for observation. I

wouldn't mind trying to keep her in a couple of weeks, if——'

'A couple of *weeks*! Surely if it's like that then she should be flown to hospital in Darwin?' Elspeth could not hide her surprise, but his explanation came quickly.

'Not for the effect of the birth and the loss. To detoxify her from the alcohol and to get a handle on whether other drugs have been involved. There was something. . .that baby. . .if it had survived it would have suffered from full Foetal Alcohol Syndrome for the rest of its life. The signs were all there—the small head, receding jaw. I'm sure you're aware of them. There's no doubt that mental retardation would have been a big factor too. I'm wondering what else she was taking in Brisbane. She's so young that there's a chance that this mess can be turned around. Florence is an excellent role model. I hope she can come in today, since she officially keeps nine-to-five hours.'

'And what hours do you keep, Lachlan?' she asked gently.

'You mean, will I hover over Nancy twenty-four hours a day for the next two weeks because of what I *couldn't* do to save her baby?'

'Something like that.'

He laughed, but didn't say anything more on the subject of overwork and they continued to drive in silence. Yesterday Ellie had been a passenger looking idly out of the window and dressed in lacy finery. Today she was the one negotiating dusty potholes in the road and slowing to cross the dry stony beds of wet-season creeks as if she had lived in the region for months, and Lachlan did not seem to think it necessary to ask her if she felt competent at the wheel. Perhaps that was a compliment.

Perhaps, on the other hand, he was already drawing her into a tight net of complete dedication to their shared medical work that would leave almost no time for the growth of their marriage. A nurse with a marriage certificate. A wife with a residence permit. With a shock, she realised that she didn't even know what would be happening to her salary out here. Was Lachlan himself authorised to write out the cheques? Or did they arrive by mail? Considering this was to be a practical marriage, there were a hundred and one practical questions they hadn't yet begun to discuss.

She looked across at Lachlan, about to ask some questions on the subject. He was leaning half against the back seat, half against the window, and his hand was over his eyes. Lower on his face, the growth of stubble already seemed thicker and darker than it had been when he arrived home from his long hours of work at Nancy Walpir's makeshift dwelling. Was he asleep? Behind him, yesterday's acacias and termite mounds flashed past in a blur and Elspeth turned her eyes quickly back to the road.

They went over a bump somewhat too fast and dust filtered into the vehicle, making her throat dry and scratchy. She glanced at him again. He was lower against the seat back. He *was* dozing. In that case, let him be. Elspeth swallowed a sudden loneliness of spirit and concentrated on the drive.

Twenty minutes later she crossed the raucous xylophone of a metal cattle grid and was inside the Nagadi boundary fence. Almost immediately she came up against a fork in the road that she had not noticed yesterday, and found that it was not signposted. Unwillingly she pulled the four-wheel-drive vehicle to a dusty halt. Lachlan still dozed, his long legs a solid diagonal across the middle of the car, which made it difficult for her to change gears.

'Lachlan?' she whispered tentatively and reached a

hand to his shoulder, noticing a film of dust streaking his collarbone beyond the opening of his blue shirt.

'Hm?' He stirred and stretched, then sat upright, the sudden alertness belied by his exhaustion-reddened eyes. He had had less than two hours' sleep last-night. 'I was asleep? Sorry.'

'This fork. I don't know which way——'

'Left. The right one leads to the main homestead where we were yesterday. Florence's family has its own place on the creek a little further downstream.'

Elspeth nodded and started forward again, swinging the wheel to the left. A few moments they pulled up in front of a neat fibro house and were greeted by a clumsy chorus of three barking dogs and two urchin boys.

Florence was in the kitchen, and an appetising yeasty smell told them that she had recently put loaves of freshly made bread into the oven to bake. She grinned at Elspeth and frowned at Lachlan. Evidently she was in no doubt about what this Sunday visit meant. 'Do I have to come now?' But her response when she had heard the story was calm and willing. 'OK, I'll come on my bike.'

She went to the back door and called the boys, who were once again scrambling in the yard with dogs and balls.

'Ernie, Tom! You boys come here, all right? Now listen. I gotta go into town and I won't be home, so you take out that bread when this clock says half-past three, or else the house'll catch fire and burn down, and Dad'll give you a real thumping you won't forget till you're ninety-five.'

The dire threat was issued in a cheerful tone that told the boys they didn't have too much to fear—although it was a strongly advisable that they *did* remember to take out the bread.

'Now I'll get my gear. Tom, you want to bring my bike round from the shed?' His grin told them all that he did. It was evidently a treat. 'Now you two get along back, Doctor Lach, and I'll be close behind.'

'Good girl, Florence.' He reached out and patted her shoulder.

She shrugged. 'Dumb old kid, Nancy Walpir. Good kid once, she was. Don't know what we're going to do with her.'

As Lachlan and Elspeth drew away, this time with Lachlan at the wheel, they saw eight-year-old Tom round the corner of the shed at a dangerous lurch, astride a small motorbike which he didn't seem yet to have fully under control. It spurted alarmingly towards the veranda of the small house then came to a halt with a puff of exhaust smoke and an ensuing silence which announced that it had stalled. Wearing a small red pack, a neat cotton uniform of pale blue check and strapping a helmet carefully on to her head, Florence emerged from the house.

An enormous goanna, streaking across the track and up a rough-barked tree and coming to rest with an impossible disregard for gravity against its vertical limbs, was the only distraction on the drive back. Lachlan was the first to see it and he pointed it out laconically: 'Goanna. Look, up the tree,' as he slowed the Toyota briefly. After this he was silent.

Elspeth remembered their long evenings of conversation in Darwin and wondered if that interlude had closed now. In a moment of bitterness that caught her by surprise she remembered Jacqueline Harcourt's bluntness and said to herself, he's got me safely here and married now. He doesn't have to bother with conversation. But no, it was ridiculous to think that way. There had been no wily design behind his actions in Darwin. He was tired today, that was all. Small wonder that chit-chat wasn't his style just at the moment.

Florence was only a few minutes behind them on her

little motorcycle, and when they reached Borragidgee Lachlan did not even bother to come inside the house. Instead, he farewelled Elspeth with what seemed like an absent-minded pat and unlocked the adjacent medical centre, where the tiny baby's body was at rest. A Flying Doctor plane would be calling in late this afternoon to take the pitiful cargo to Darwin, where an autopsy would confirm and amplify Lachlan's theories about why the baby had not survived to be born.

Ellie, back at her unpacking, heard the Toyota start up again as Lachlan and Florence set off for the shack on the outskirts of town where Nancy was being tended in a primitive but loving fashion by her grandmother and an aunt.

Loneliness descended once more, not because Lachlan was physically absent from her but because so much of his energy was elsewhere, and no matter how much she told herself that it was understandable and right on this day of tragic emergency, Ellie felt abandoned. Ridiculously she thought of Jackie Harcourt again. Where did the English journalist live? She had no idea. As if she would go and pay a visit even if she knew! How unbearably, wickedly interested Jackie would be in the fact that a medical emergency had separated the newly-weds for most of the day following their wedding!

With a firm rein on her feelings, Elspeth made herself coffee, finished her unpacking, then studied the contents of the kitchen for clues as to what she could begin to prepare for their evening meal. It was as she spread a final layer of grated mozzarella and parmesan cheese on to the savoury marconi cheese she had prepared that she heard voices in the medical centre. Quickly she switched on the electric oven and slipped the stoneware casserole dish inside, then took her keys, unlocked the connecting door that led from the central passageway and went uncertainly through. Would she be wanted? There were two female voices as well as Lachlan's. That meant that Florence had succeeded in persuading Nancy to come in.

Elspeth caught Lachlan just as he was slipping out through the front door. 'The Flying Doctor plane will be landing any minute, and I don't want to keep them waiting,' he said. 'I have to get out to the airstrip.'

'All right. Will you be. . .' But he was away before she could finish the sentence, carrying the wrapped bundle and the case notes he had quickly scribbled about the mother's poor pre-natal care and the baby's sadly unlived life. '. . .home for dinner?' Elspeth finished the sentence lamely, delivering it to thin air. Surely he would be home. It wasn't as if there was anywhere else in Borragidgee he could go for a meal, anywhere public, that is, and he was hardly likely to be invited into someone's house the day after his wedding.

She went through to where Florence was helping Nancy in the small bathroom that adjoined the tiny three-bed ward which was their 'hospital'. Together they sponged the girl, who looked thin and unhealthy and even younger than her sixteen years. She was very quiet, muttering a few words to Florence but only staring down when Elspeth stood beside her, refusing to make contact out of the black glazed-looking pools that were her eyes. She seemed uneasy and reluctant when once stretched out beneath the crisp white sheets too, and Ellie could detect no reply to Florence's questioning, 'Cuppa tea?'

Somehow, though, Florence interpreted the lack of response as a 'yes', and went to the medical centre's kitchen to put on the kettle. Ellie set up a chart for Nancy and negotiated the unfamiliar filing system successfully in order to find the girl's file, then took a routine set of observations—temperature, blood-pressure and pulse. She found that each fell within the normal range, noted them down and then followed Florence to the kitchen.

'What's done about meals when we have a patient in overnight?'

'Mrs Dyer, you know; she and Jack Dyer run the store?'

'Yes, I. . .perhaps I met them yesterday.' The names sounded faintly familiar. Yesterday seemed like weeks ago.

'We tell her we've got someone and she brings over their food.'

'Has she been told yet about Nancy?'

'No, that's something I've got to do.'

'I'll make the tea, then, shall I? If you'd like to go now?'

Florence nodded, taking it as an instruction, which wasn't quite what Elspeth meant and she felt a bit awkward. Florence was far more at home here than she was herself at this stage. But the Aboriginal girl went off down the street to the store, not thinking that anything was amiss. Elspeth made the tea and took it in to Nancy, who reached out her hand for the cup silently, and again without making eye contact.

Reluctant to leave her alone, but not wanting to make it obvious that she was keeping watch, Ellie manufactured some unnecessary tasks out in the main office area of the medical centre until Florence returned.

'Mrs Dyer says she'll be over at seven with a hot meal. Dr Lach said you weren't to work today so I'm sending you next door now.' She grinned.

'Next door?'

'Yes, to your place. The house. Dr Lach's house.'

'Oh, of course.' Ellie felt foolish at her own slowness but departed without protest, a tiny ember of warmth glowing in her at the fact that Lachlan had wanted to protect her from being caught up in the work environment this first day. In the kitchen the macaroni cheese was starting to smell deliciously savoury and Elspeth found that it was already six o'clock. She found some salad things in the fridge and tossed up a bowl of lettuce, tomato and green pepper with an improvised vinegar dressing. Lachlan should be back at any minute. . .

But the macaroni cheese was threatening to dry out and burn before he finally appeared, entering through the passage that led to the medical centre. He had checked on his patient first. As it should be, of course.

'Ellie! What do I smell? Have you made dinner?'

'Yes, I——'

'That's great!' He stepped forward and for a moment it looked as if he was going to swirl her into his arms and crush her warmly against him, but then he stopped in mid-track, looked away at a patch of floor and added unnecessarily, 'That's very nice of you. And a salad, too.'

'How's Nancy?'

'Asleep. She's exhausted. That should keep her firmly in place for tonight, at least. Want to sit on the veranda and I'll bring you a drink?'

'That sounds lovely. You were longer than I thought you'd be.' She couldn't help adding the last words, finding her place in this domestic scene with difficulty.

'Yes.' He shifted his feet restlessly. 'I ran into Jackie Harcourt at the airstrip.' He didn't elaborate, but pressed a hand to her shoulder to coax her out to the veranda. 'What can I get you? Something long and cool? Brandy and ginger ale with a slice of lemon?'

'Sounds lovely,' she managed, still dwelling on his casual reference to Jacqueline Harcourt; then she remembered the macaroni cheese. 'But I should turn off the oven.'

She turned back and met the wall of his chest, too

quickly for him to step aside. It seemed as if he didn't want to step aside, either, since his arms closed around her and she felt his lips nuzzling her thick hair, loosening the combs she had hurriedly placed there several hours ago.

'Mmm, Ellie. . .' His hands moved on her back, making her flesh melt, but there was a stiffness to him as if he wasn't quite sure why he was touching her. One of the combs clattered to the floor with the brittle sound of plastic and gave her the excuse to pull away, although her treacherous body told her to stay there and rediscover the pleasure of his touch.

'Oops. . .' She gave a breathy laugh and bent down for the comb, fumbling awkwardly. Before she stood up again he had left her and was busy in the kitchen. As she walked with cotton-wool legs out to the veranda, she heard cupboard doors opening and shutting, glasses clinking, and the cool sigh of the fridge closing.

Why had that moment in his arms confused her? Perhaps it was only under the cover of darkness that she felt safe in his arms and could forget about her doubts as to *why* she was there. Or was it the recent mention of Jackie Harcourt, slipped in casually and not followed through? 'I met Jackie at the airstrip.' The English journalist had delayed him, then, but Lachlan hadn't explained how.

Forget about it, Ellie told herself. It's unimportant. She found a striped canvas easy-chair on the veranda and sat back in it, willing herself to relax as if she had come home after a long day of nursing duties. Instead, though, her impulse was to sit upright waiting nervously for Lachlan feeling like an early guest at a cocktail party—a little tense and uncertain, worried that the host was secretly wishing no one had arrived for another half an hour.

When he came out five minutes later she had closed

her eyes and so she couldn't tell if he noticed how unnaturally posed she was for someone who was supposedly resting. She heard the chink of ice as Lachlan put her drink down on the small cane and glass table next to her, then the creak of canvas as he settled into the easychair that was the twin of her own. She opened her eyes and found that he was watching her.

'I'm glad to escape from that kitchen,' he said teasingly. 'The smell coming from the oven was so delicious I nearly abandoned the drinks.'

'It's only macaroni cheese,' she blurted.

'Oh yes,' he laughed, 'an old stand-by of my own, but it always tastes twice as good when someone else has done the work. Thank you for that.'

'Oh, it was no trouble. I like cooking,' she answered vaguely.

'It's not possible to be a gourmet out here, unfortunately,' he said. 'Too much is unavailable.'

'Oh, I like plain cooking as much as fancy things.'

Their conversation continued in this bland vein until it lapsed into silence, apparently because neither of them was certain whether the other one wanted to continue. After an uncomfortable few minutes Lachlan picked up the newspaper that lay folded on the lower shelf of the two-tiered cane coffee-table and passed the magazine section to Elspeth.

'There's an interesting article in there about. . .er. . .travel in Alaska,' he said absently.

'Is there?'

'And other things, of course.' He waved his hand vaguely, and then settled down to read.

Elspeth opened the magazine and dutifully turned to the article about travel in Alaska, but the black newsprint blurred before her eyes and she could only sit and wonder what was wrong. It should be perfectly possible for two married people to sit together reading and not speaking on a veranda, protected from the sunset surge of insects by flyscreens and surrounded by a pleasant array of potted plants. Why did the silence not feel harmonious?

Because we were married *yesterday*, came the answer. We should be cuddled up together on that cane sofa with the fat cushions over there, whispering and laughing together in our own language of love.

But they weren't in love. The romance was missing. Somehow, Elspeth hadn't pictured all the day-to-day moments when this would matter. . .

A woman that she faintly recognised from yesterday's now hollow-seeming celebration came diagonally across the deserted street, carrying a plastic tray laden with covered dishes: Roma Dyer bringing Nancy her meal. She had greying sandy hair that escaped untidily from a puffy French roll, and her motherly figure moved a little clumsily in the orange trousers and striped blouse.

She shook her head energetically as Elspeth made a move to get up, clearly wanting to leave the newly married couple in peace. Ellie sank back into her chair and picked up the almost empty drink and her unread magazine. Then she caught Mrs Dyer's surprised and expressive stare. Clearly she and Jack Dyer hadn't done much reading on their honeymoon. By the time Roma had disappeared into the medical centre, Ellie was flushing hotly. The general store in a small town like this was always the centre of gossip. The whole of Borragidgee would probably be talking about it tomorrow—if Jackie Harcourt didn't have them talking about it already.

Impatiently she downed the last mouthfuls of her drink at one long gulp and got to her feet. 'The dinner will be ruined if I don't serve it soon,' she said.

It came out blunt and angry, like the accusation of a long-disillusioned wife when her husband was late home to dinner, although she hadn't meant it to sound this way at all; but she was inside the house before Lachlan had had time to react. Elspeth heard only an odd exclamation break from his lips and she did not stop to respond to it.

They barely spoke to one another for the rest of the evening, sitting in a silence not hostile at all, but not satisfying either; and yet, once again, when darkness cocooned them together among the cool sheets of the wide bed, and Florence and Nancy were both quietly sleeping in the medical centre attached to the far end of the house, their lovemaking filled the night with a mounting turmoil of sensation that left Elspeth numb and swollen with awareness and completion.

CHAPTER FIVE

'LACHLAN not here, then?'

'No, Peter, he's out at Barton Downs all morning,' Ellie answered as she examined the lump at the back of his neck that had brought him in.

It was a bright Tuesday, full of the unvarying sunlight of the dry season, unsullied by humidity. Florence had gone with Lachlan out to Barton Downs, and Leonie, the youngest of the three health workers, sat in the ward where Nancy was still under observation. Physically, the trauma of childbirth had left her very much unscathed in spite of her long labour. She had needed no stitches and the muscles of her pelvic floor had not been unduly strained. Lachlan had decided against giving her any medication to stem the flow of her unneeded breast milk.

'It stops soon enough on its own,' he had said. 'As long as we guard against infection, I'd rather not dose her up with bromocryptine. If she's in pain from engorgement, of course we'll give an analgesic.'

Still, however, it was other aspects of Nancy's condition which gave more concern. She was quiet and withdrawn and even Florence hadn't been able to draw her out. In addition, her aunt and grandmother had been caught during a brief visit yesterday morning supplying her with cigarettes and even a bottle of whisky. They had looked sheepish and ashamed when found out, and a heated conversation had taken place in their tribal language afterwards when they were left alone with Nancy. They had not been back to visit since, although Lachlan had wanted to encourage them.

Occasionally Leonie could be heard chatting to Nancy

84

in their softly musical mother tongue, but mostly the reply, if any was inaudible.

'Sorry to bother you with a stupid thing like this,' Peter Dane was saying. 'I held off yesterday, but it's worrying me a bit so I thought, hang it, it's not as if my coming'll make much difference to the time you two get to be by yourselves.'

Elspeth made a token answer then focused her attention more carefully on the mysterious lump. It was only a cyst but in the dusty air of the outback, and with Peter spending much of his day among cattle, it could easily become infected, so she swabbed it carefully with antiseptic, applied a small amount of pressure to drain it gently and easily, swabbed it again and then covered with a band-aid.

Peter laughed ruefully when she explained the problem. 'Kate—my brother's wife—panicked and thought it was an insect bite gone bad. I've wasted half a morning now. She could have done what you just did. I should have just radioed in and tried to describe it, but since it was clinic day. . .at least I've used the trip to pick up some supplies as well.'

'Keep an eye on it all the same. You must all be tired after the party on Saturday,' Ellie said. 'All that work. Perhaps that's why Kate over-reacted. I. . .we appreciated it so much.'

'Any excuse for a get-together out here,' he answered her off-handedly. 'We'd have found another reason soon enough if it hadn't been for you two. Give my best to Lachlan when he gets back.'

'I will,' she promised casually, wondering if her husband would ask about the morning's patients or whether he would simply look at the files she left on his desk. Two days a week were enough to set aside in this small town for regular clinic hours, and most people didn't even bother to make an appointment. If things were busy, people were always happy to wait and chat to anyone else who was around or to pop along the street to visit Jack and Roma Dyer in the store.

When Peter Dane had gone, Elspeth tidied the surgery and office area restlessly, placing already neatly arranged charts and files in an even neater pile and disposing meticulously of the cotton swabs she had used to treat Peter's cyst. She wished Lachlan would return, somehow feeling that the next time she saw him she would find a way to say. . .what? She didn't know, but it couldn't be only her imagination that insisted that the gap between them that had opened imperceptibly since Saturday night was widening.

While she had slept late on Monday morning, he had quietly got up and gone to check on Florence and Nancy. The former had then gone home to help the boys get ready for school, and Lachlan had given Annie instructions on Nancy's care for the rest of the morning. Ellie, in a half-doze, had scarcely been aware of his return to bed, although her body had instinctively relaxed and shaped itself against the cradle of his arms.

The cocoon of sleep and warmth had been beginning to give way to the sharper and richer awareness of desire in both of them when the buzzer connected to the radio equipment had sounded. Lachlan had gone from her almost before she fully became aware of what the instrusive sound meant and later, on dressing and going to the medical centre, she had heard from Annie that the Flying Doctor Service had asked him to check on a minor emergency at the mines thirty miles to the north-west, since both their planes were out on other calls and would be late on the scene.

It had been lunchtime before he had returned; then in the afternoon he had visited the shanty where Nancy's aunt and grandmother lived to try and talk to them about Nancy's life in Brisbane and her problem with alcohol, tobacco and other drugs. It hadn't been a very productive session, apparently, although it wasn't that the two women were hostile. There should be a way, Ellie knew, for him to pour out more of his preoccupation with Nancy, and she groped for the right questions but could not find them.

Today, Tuesday, when he returned from Barton Downs just after lunch, she greeted him with an indrawn breath, poised to utter a sentence that surely ought to be on the tip of her tongue, the right thing to draw them together, and yet she could not think of what it was. He looked at her oddly. 'Hello, Ellie. Nothing wrong, is there?'

'No, it's been an ordinary morning.' And the moment passed.

Until four, the afternoon was quiet, and then the rattle of an old open-backed land-rover in the driveway announced another patient. More than one, apparently. Four people, all Aboriginal, filed into the tiny waiting-room that adjoined the office. Elspeth, alone over some paper-work at that moment while Lachlan checked on Nancy Walpir, gave them all a friendly greeting, then asked, 'To see the doctor? All of you?'

A well-built man of middle years came forward. He hesitated and looked back at the group in the waiting-chairs, then said, 'No, just Granny Alice, here. Doc said a couple of weeks ago we should bring her in soon. She's been falling again.'

The old woman sat staring down at the hands she had pressed between her thin knees. A floral dress hung loosely on her, and her bent frame told Elspeth that she had been a woman of good height and build in her youth, but was now shrunken from the decalcification of age.

'Falling down, Granny Alice, are you?' Granny Alice looked up when she heard this address and grinned at Elspeth, who smiled back.

An old man who could have been the woman's husband stared vaguely at Ellie, too. From the distance at which she stood, there looked to be something funny about his eyes, but Elspeth couldn't make out what it was. In any case, the younger man had said it was only Granny Alice who wanted looking at. Evidently the others had simply come along for the ride into town. With the complex kin systems in Aboriginal culture, none of them were necessarily close relatives, either. It was a warm and open sort of arrangement, with the sharing of worldly possessions an understood thing, but it could be confusing.

Then the younger woman spoke, 'Uncle Bill. . .'

The old man turned to look at her, although his eyes seemed out of focus. 'Hm? What are you saying to me?'

'Aren't you going to get Dr Lach to take a look at your eyes?'

'My eyes don't hurt, girl.'

'I know they don't hurt, but you can hardly see any more. You've got that film over them. You went walkabout the last couple of times he was out our way, didn't you? On purpose! I know you, you old so-and-so. . .and so he didn't get to see them.'

'That what you wanted me to come in for?'

'No, Uncle Bill, it was your idea to come in because you wanted to buy your chocolate biscuits and see Albert Bunurri if he's home when we go past, remember?'

As they talked, Ellie realised what it was that she could not make out distinctly from the far side of the waiting area: the old man—Uncle Bill—had the grey film of cataracts hazing over the black brilliance of his large eyes. They would have grown gradually and probably seemed to old Bill just another symptom of his failing health, although he seemed much more upright and alert than old Granny Alice.

If the cataracts 'didn't hurt' he probably hadn't even

thought that something could be done. No doubt his only contact with the world of medicine had been the relief of acute pain in the past—perhaps a broken limb reset or a griping appendix removed. Perhaps not even that much. He looked as healthy as his age allowed—sure of his place in the world too, with none of the signs of the habitual drinker.

'Why don't you see Dr Lach?' Ellie said with careful good humour. 'He's not busy this afternoon and I'm sure he'd like to say hello. . . Here he is now.'

She turned as the door that led to the tiny ward area opened and Lachlan entered, almost filling the height of the frame with his capable length. It was the first time she had used the 'Dr Lach' that so many of the Borragidgee people, including Roma Dyer, seemed to favour. It felt like a trespass, a nickname she hadn't earned the right to bandy around yet.

'Uncle Bill Namadja!' he was saying. 'Yes, I *would* like to say hello. How are you, Bill?' He came forward and shook the old man's hand heartily. Bill had stood up to greet the doctor and Ellie knew, although she couldn't have said how, that Lachlan had noticed the cataracts at once. Perhaps he hadn't been altogether surprised, either. He might have noticed them beginning to grow during an earlier encounter with Bill Namadja. 'Let's go into my office and have a talk. I've got tea, and there's even a chocolate biscuit or two, I think.' Evidently these were well known as being the old man's vice.

The younger woman, who name Ellie didn't know, spoke up. 'Mrs McLintock, mind if we go over to the store while we're waiting? Granny Alice'll be all right with you, won't she?'

'I'm sure she will,' Ellie nodded, while the words 'Mrs McLintock' echoed strangely in her mind. 'Go ahead.'

'You're nice and quiet today, aren't you, Granny Alice?'

'Yes, I'm good, I'm OK,' the old woman said, nodding repeatedly.

The two younger people left without fuss as if Granny Alice might want to go along too once she realised they were leaving her. Elspeth was just about to offer her the ubiquitous outback welcome of a cup of tea when the outer door pushed abruptly open and a flash of yellow shirt and turquoise trousers brought Jacqueline Harcourt into the room.

'Granny Alice!' she exclaimed with loud delight. 'It *was* your nephew Charlie's jeep I saw parked outside. . . Hello, Elspeth.'

Ellie replied politely enough to the appended greeting but she was watching this treatment of the old Aboriginal woman warily.

'Granny Alice!' the journalist said again, still loudly. 'It's good to see you!'

Granny Alice looked more animated and smiled, and Elspeth wondered if she herself had been speaking too softly to the old woman, who seemed to be grateful for Jackie's loud tones.

'I had the most wonderful time with you last week, Granny Alice,' the journalist was saying. 'The stories you told and the place you showed me. I felt very. . .privileged, lucky. . .that you trusted me so much. Do you remember that we're going to go out again and you're going to tell me more of the ancient women's lore?'

'What? I showed you?' Granny Alice looked both roused and confused now; agitated too. 'What're you saying, missus?'

'Jackie. I'm Jackie, remember?'

'Yeah, I remember you.'

'Well, we're going to see each other again, aren't we? That's what I'm saying.'

'Yeah, OK, all right. We'll see each other. That's good.' Her brief energy lapsed into dullness again.

Elspeth, busying herself in the background with tea-making, realised that Granny Alice must be the woman who had 'intuitively responded' to Jackie last week out at Walgunya, the Aboriginal cattle station. The words were clearly a journalistic exaggeration. Judging by her condition today, the old woamn had probably been confused rather than responsive to Jackie's energetic attempt at friendship. It was self-deception on the journalist's part to say the least, and Ellie wondered what Jackie was hoping to get out of the relationship. Some startling revelation for the book, no doubt. It seemed unlikely that she would succeed.

A one-sided conversation continued between Jackie and Granny Alice as Elspeth gave them both tea, but then the old woman retreated even further into herself, merely mumbling into her steaming cup, and Jackie gave up her efforts and came over, instead, to Elspeth.

'She's really marvellous, actually,' the English journalist said in a low, confidential voice. 'She seems confused and quiet today, but last week she was so responsive.'

'Was she? That's good,' Ellie smiled non-committally, and not fully convinced.

'It's just a matter of drawing her out in the right way, and of course she's better in her own environment. That's what journalism is all about.'

'Yes, I'm sure that's true.'

'I must have you two over to dinner in my little caravan soon, but I'm going out to the Radnor Mining headquarters at the end of the week, so. . .would Thursday night be too soon to trespass on your togetherness?'

Ellie was thrown off track by the last words, wondering if she was right to suspect a trace of irony, and was just bringing out a clumsy couple of phrases about 'asking Lachlan' and 'talking over our schedule' when he came out of his office, ushering Uncle Bill Namadja in front of him.

'Jackie!' he said heartily, his Scottish accent strong and his voice clear and resonant. 'Thought I heard your voice.'

It wasn't his usual manner, Ellie decided. What was it about the English journalist that seemed to bring out in him a repertoire of voice tones and mannerisms that with others she didn't see in him?

'Elspeth and I were just talking about the possibility of dinner on Thursday at my caravan,' Jackie was saying. 'Is it all right with you?'

'Er. . .yes, I think so.' He glanced across at Ellie and frowned. Was he expecting her to say something? Jackie's words made it sound as if Elspeth had already virtually accepted the invitation.

'I said——' Ellie began, but before she could finish '—that I'd ask you,' Lachlan had continued more positively.

'Yes, it sounds fine. What time?'

'Elspeth?' Jackie turned to her.

'Oh, whatever's usual up here,' she stammered, not really wanting to go at all, or not so soon. 'Seven?'

'Seven it is, then. . . And now, I was wondering if Annie was about?'

'No, she isn't, Jackie,' Lachlan answered. 'Only Leonie's here.' He waved a hand abstractedly in the direction of the three-bed ward and then focused his attention on the doorway as Charlie and his woman companion re-entered carrying a bag of supplies which Elspeth could see contained numerous packets of chocolate biscuits.

'I'm glad you're back, Charlie,' Lachlan said. 'Can I see you for a moment?' His words cut across the sound of Charlie deliberately crackling the brittle plastic wrap of a biscuit packet.

Bill cocked his ears at the sound and then grinned.

'You got my biscuits?' It was significant that he had responded instantly to the aural cue but hadn't been able to see the biscuit packets that poked very obviously from the top of the paper shopping bag.

'Don't you eat them all on the way home, you old sugar-tooth,' Charlie said, as he followed Lachlan into the office.

Jackie made a quick getaway as soon as Lachlan had disappeared again, and Elspeth wondered a little about her interest in seeing Annie. Tied in with the all-important book, she presumed.

Granny Alice began to speak tetchily. 'Dorothy, when we going home? Charlie said we were going home.'

'We haven't see Dr Lach yet, Granny Alice,' the younger woman replied.

'Yes, we've seen him; that was him just now. He's just been talking with Uncle Bill.'

It took the rest of Charlie's short consultation with Lachlan for Dorothy to talk the old lady into staying calmly where she was and finishing her tea. Elspeth went to take Nancy Walpir's routine observations, and when she came back, after spending a bit of time with Leonie and their one resident patient, the four visitors had departed and their jeep could be heard starting up outside.

Lachlan's door was slightly ajar and she dared a quick peep through. He sat there at the desk with his back to her, the swivel-chair swung around and tilted back slightly so that he could rest his head against hands folded behind his neck. Ellie heard a deep sigh hiss from between his clenched teeth, then focused on the lacing of tanned fingers that had brought such swelling delight to her body in the darkness of their bed.

The breath caught in her throat and she lost the courage to go in to him. Stepping backwards, she realised it was too late to retreat. He had heard the sound of her indrawn-breath and the swivel chair had spun round with a brief, strident squeak. He stared at her with narrow eyes and slowly took his hands from behind his head, straightened up and rested splayed fingers on the desk in front of him.

'Everything all right, Ellie?'

'I was going to ask you the same question.'

'Were you?' He seemed pleased that she had noticed his mood, but then he frowned again. 'It's written on me like a newspaper headline, I suppose?'

'Page one, feature story,' she quipped, then bit her lip. Did the journalistic joke mean that Jackie Harcourt was occupying both their thoughts? 'What is it?'

He shrugged without answering, and she felt shut out. Should she leave? No. Should she have the courage to probe him a little further? Tentatively she moved forward and eased into the chair beside the desk which was placed there for patients' use. But before she could fully relax into the seat he had risen from his own chair and come around the desk, pulling her to her feet and taking her in his arms with a gentle, distant touch like that of a family friend.

Ellie held herself motionless, almost rigid, fighting her awareness of his body against hers, touching as they had been last night and as they slept. Perhaps he sensed her wariness. At any rate, he did not tighten his grip, saying quickly and carefully, 'This isn't how I wanted your first few days here to be.'

'Isn't it?'

'No, of course not. Plunged into a set of problems like this, shut out by my own preoccupation. Bill Namadja won't hear about the idea of surgery for his cataracts even though he's a tribal elder with many good years left in him yet. Granny Alice is getting so confused and unpredictable. Her falls are dangerous, and she wanders off into the bush without telling anyone, ending up miles from help. Then there's Nancy, of course. . . I'd been hoping for a week of tourists with chickenpox or beefy stockmen with cut thumbs.'

'Jackie seems to feel that Granny Alice is very lucid a good deal of the time,' Ellie put in.

'I know,' he frowned. 'Jackie. . .' He sighed, saying the name on an odd note as if the journalist too was a problem. 'You'll prosecute me for false advertising. I was far more relaxed in Darwin. I'm not like this all the time.'

'I'm sure you're not.' She didn't like the tense apology, feeling unsure of the response he wanted from her.

'Listen. . .' He released her suddenly and took a restless pace into the room. 'We'll shut up shop tomorrow and go up to the south boundary of Walkadu. . .take a picnic. . .stay all day.'

'You don't have to do that just for me,' she began.

'Who says I'm doing it for you?' he growled in reply, and at last they both laughed and Elspeth felt the tension lift.

'Aren't you on permanent call, though?'

'I am. We both are. But we'll have the Toyota with the radio, and Florence will be in all day with Nancy.'

He became practical again and seemed to have shaken off some of his darkly self-condemning mood. They talked about the day, and Elspeth got answers to some of the work-related questions she had been storing up. It was a level she realised—one of the levels—on which they related well to one another.

'And now,' he said finally, 'I'm going to make you a proper evening meal.' They had eaten *ad hoc* last night, just tinned lentil soup and toasted sandwiches.

'We can cook together,' she offered quickly, enjoying the prospect of sharing a practical task with him.

But he shook his head. 'If you don't mind, I'd like you to potter round in here a bit longer. Annie's due in at six to stay with Nancy until morning. Leonie's the least experienced of the three and she can't necessarily be relied upon to know when to come and call one of us. All three girls are doing so well this week, working extra hours, and the last thing I'd want is for Leonie to suspect she's not fully trusted. She'd probably get frightened and simply stop turning up for work. Could you bear to. . .make some coffee and read a medical journal as if it was simply too absorbing for you to put down?'

'You mean you don't *always* read medical journals that way?' Elspeth queried with mock horror and was rewarded with his rich, open laugh—a laugh that she had heard rarely, she realised, apart from their time in Darwin. She added quickly: 'Of course I don't mind.'

A few minutes later she was alone at the desk that separated office area from waiting-room and had, in fact, found an article which interested her. She decided to read for a while then take a break to make coffee and incidentally poke her head around the ward door on her way to the kitchen. She was interrupted in her reading, however, by suddenly becoming aware that Leonie was standing there watching her gravely and shyly.

'Oh, Leonie! You gave me a bit of a fright.'

'Sorry, Sister.'

'That's all right. It's just that you were so quiet coming in.'

'Nancy says she's ready to go home now,' Leonie announced next in her shy way, and as if Elspeth would have been expecting this news.

'Home? Oh, no, she's not going home yet.'

'Isn't she?'

'No. Mrs Dyer will be coming over soon with her dinner, and then Annie'll be here to stay with her overnight. You go back and tell her her dinner's coming soon.'

'OK.' Leonie turned obediently and went back along

the corridor. Ellie watched her, frowning and wishing she'd handled the situation a little differently. She should have found a way to get up and go to Nancy herself to find out just what was going on. If she followed Leonie now it would betray the distrust that Lachlan had been so concerned about.

Restlessly she remained seated, listening for voices and activity down the corridor. She heard a bit of conversation but no unexplainable sounds, and had just gone back to her reading when Leonie appeared again, as shyly and silently as before.

'Nancy says she's not hungry this evening.'

'Isn't she? But she's all right now, is she? Everything's all right?'

Leonie stepped back a pace, as if Elspeth's tone had been too demanding. 'Yes, everything's all right,' she said, then lapsed into a much-used Australian idiom. 'No worries, Sister, no worries.'

'All right, then, Leonie; well, you go back and look after her, but come and tell me as soon as you or she need me for any reason, OK? Come if you need me.'

'OK. . .' The girl padded silently away, and again Elspeth wondered if she should have said or done something different.

To assuage her doubts she got up and went to the medical centre's kitchen to prepare some coffee, glancing quickly to her left as she passed the open ward door. Nancy had gone to the bathroom, it seemed. A flushing sound came from behind the closed bathroom door, and Leonie stood by herself next to Nancy's bed.

As Ellie spooned coffee into a shiny brown mug and waited for the small electric kettle to boil, she went on listening to the sounds coming from the ward: the pad of Nancy's bare feet, the creak of the bed. Nothing to worry about there. No smell of cigarette smoke as there had been a couple of times, either. Coffee in hand, she returned to her desk and, hearing voices in the girls' shared tribal tongue, she didn't even glance into the room.

It was good that Nancy was talking, opening up a little out of her withdrawn, sullen silence. Eye contact with the young girl could break the new growth of communication. If Nancy talked like this to Florence tomorrow, Lachlan would be pleased. . .

Sipping her coffee, Elspeth heard a sudden clatter of pans that was loud enough to cross the two closed doors between the office and Lachlan's kitchen. *Their* kitchen, of course. Her heart went out to him suddenly, and she wondered what he was preparing for their meal. He had made it sound as if he was making a special effort, and she found that she wanted to contribute, to make it a shared thing. With tomorrow's picnic planned and the consequent sense of holiday, it could be their first really special meal, perhaps with wine. And dessert.

On impulse she put down the half-finished coffee and stood up. It would only take a moment to cross the road and cover the fifty yards to the Dyers' store. They ought to have something. . .even if it was only another packet of Bill Namadja's beloved chocolate biscuits. And she could warn Roma that Nancy might be reluctant about eating her meal tonight. Annie would need to be told that, too. It was important for Nancy to eat a balanced meal.

These thoughts got her out of the medical centre, down the steps and halfway across the street. At the cluttered store it was Jack Dyer behind the counter. He was 'yarning' with a mate and, although he included Elspeth in the conversation, it was a few minutes before she could break the flow to tell him what she wanted.

The outback disregard for time! God made plenty of it, she had heard a bush-bred patient say at Royal Northern Hospital. She had forgotten about the leisurely pace of the Dyers' when embarking on her impulsive errand.

'Something for dessert?' Jack said when she had finally given her request. 'Yes, we've got some of these frozen things here somewhere.'

'Oh, ice-cream? No, we have that already.'

'No, not ice-cream, love, those frozen pies and things you heat up in the oven.'

'Really? That would be lovely.'

'Well, we've got lots of different ones.' He went through a door in the back of the shop, opened the lid of a huge white freezer unit that stood in the store-room and rummaged among the contents. Vapour rose, floated and sank again around him. 'Let's see, there's. . . What's this called? Cinnamon Apple Strudel,' he announced slowly with elaborate care. 'Apricot Danish. New York Cheesecake. Can't read this one, it's all frosted over. Better check the "Use By" date on that in a minute. Now, this next one. . . Hearty Cherry Pie.'

'That sounds fine,' Elspeth said, beginning to be quite agitated at the length of her absence. If Lachlan came into the office and found her gone, this delightful surprise could turn into a tension-filled-let-down.

'We've got other things, love. What's this, now? Oh, another cheesecake. But let's see. . .'

'Cherry pie is fine, honestly,' she repeated desperately. 'You're sure?'

'Yes, positive,' she nodded energetically and to her relief he closed the freezer lid with a muffled bump and came back with a square cardboard box.

Ellie reached quickly for her purse. . .and realised that she'd forgotten to bring it. 'Oh, crikey! I didn't bring any money!' she exclaimed in anguish, but at this he only laughed.

'I'll chalk it up for you, love, don't worry.'

'Will you? Thanks so much, this is just what I needed.

And I'll see Roma when she comes over with Nancy's meal. I can pay her then,' she gabbled, breathless and grateful, and then made a getaway that was, by outback standards, rudely abrupt.

Back at the medical centre, she burst through the door expecting to see an angry Lachlan or an anxious Leonie, but the office was empty and the ward down the corridor was quiet. Annie should be here within fifteen minutes, and Roma Dyer soon after that.

With a gusty sigh of relief Ellie put the box, now covered with a film of frost, on her desk and returned to lukewarm coffee and magazine. She would take the Hearty Cherry Pie into Lachlan when she was finished in here; then perhaps she'd shower and change and make some hors d'oeuvres to have with a brandy and ginger ale. . .

Leonie was in front of her again.

'Everything all right, Leonie?'

'Yes, everything's good. No worries.'

'Nancy's good?'

'Yes, she's good,' the girl nodded cheerfully. 'She's gone home now.'

CHAPTER SIX

'WHAT?' The urgently shouted word brought immediate fear into Leonie's eyes.

'She went home,' she repeated. 'She's all right now. She's not sick. She didn't want to stay here any more. That's all.'

I can't deal with this on my own, Elspeth realised, weak at the knees. I'm angry with myself. Should I be angry with Leonie as well?

Lachlan would have to be called, and at once. . .

'You're angry with me, aren't you?' she said to him in the main office ten minutes later.

Leonie had gone home, melting away without saying goodnight, and Annie, just arrived, had been sent across the road to tell Roma Dyer to hold back on the meal, although hopefully it would be needed later if they got Nancy back again. The autopsy report had come through from Darwin that morning and it showed what they had expected—several internal problems in the baby as well as a more detailed summary of all the external signs that pointed to damage *in utero* through maternal drug-abuse. A specialist in Adelaide would be using some of the information as part of his research into drug use and perinatal death within the Aboriginal population. Meanwhile, here at Borragidgee, they had only just begun to deal with Nancy's problems.

'Yes, I *am* angry with you,' Lachlan said, pacing the room restlessly. His hands were thrust into khaki trouser pockets, as if he was afraid that the force of his anger might unleash itself, and his square, strong shoulders were held as tense and rigid as iron bars. 'No. . . Should I be angry? I can't help it.'

'I'm angry with myself,' Elspeth put in steadily.

Her heart was thudding. She hadn't seen him like this before. There was something bold and almost over-powering in his anger. It was strong, direct, unashamed, yet controlled at the same time. His blue eyes glittered restlessly and she could tell that his mind was ticking away even as it was gripped by emotion, seeking a course of action to solve the problem.

The cardboard box containing the cherry pie was growing soft and soggy as it thawed, leaving a small moat of water around itself as it still sat on Elspeth's desk.

'Let's not waste any more time,' Lachlan said. 'We'll go round there on the off-chance. . .'

'I don't understand, Lachlan.'

'Her aunt and grandmother understood in the end, after I'd talked to them yesterday, exactly why I wanted Nancy in here. She'd bullied them into bringing the alcohol. . .'

'Bullied? Nancy?'

'Oh, yes, she's not always as quiet as you've seen her. Anyway, they agreed she had more of a chance here than at home. I doubt she's gone there, but I don't know where else to try. They might at least be able to give us some ideas. . .'

Annie came back from the Dyers' and was put in charge of the medical centre—although the health work-ers were not permitted to handle any complex equipment or have access to medication of any kind—while Lachlan and Elspeth climbed into the Toyota and made the short journey to the outskirts of town.

Lachlan's anger seemed more contained now that his energy was directed towards action, but Elspeth thought painfully of the chicken casserole that had been simmer-ing on the stove when she had brought him the news about Nancy, and the mouth-watering smell of herb and garlic bread that had been coming from the oven. The stove would be cooling now, the casserole lukewarm, and even when they finally ate the meal it wouldn't have the special, celebratory quality she had been yearning for and counting on.

Several shack-like dwellings had grown up beside the road that petered out at this end of town. None of them was very tidy or well-kept but all had warm yellow light spilling from within as dusk overtook the dessert land, and the riotous laughter of children came from two verandas. The Walpir house was one of the quietest.

Nancy wasn't there. Lachlan nodded without visible emotion at the news while Elspeth stood behind him in silence. A stew boiling on the old, slightly sloping stove reminded her again of the uneaten meal at home, and although Nancy's aunt and grandmother joined together to invite them in to tea Lachlan shook his head.

'Anywhere else in town she might have gone?' he asked.

'I don't know. I don't know,' said the older woman, Kath, rubbing her dry hands together with a rough, papery sound.

'She'll be at Bradley's if she's anywhere,' the aunt, Lou, said on a worried, vinegary note. 'I'd say, anyway. At Bradley's.'

'Bradley's?' Kath repeated. 'Yeah, that's right. Bad boy in the family, part of what got her going wrong in the first place. He's in the jail now, in Darwin.'

'Jail?' Lachlan barked. 'What for?'

'Him and another bloke, fighting in a pub. Real bad. Sister's nice. Nancy'd be there, I reckon, if she was anywhere.'

But Nancy was not at Bradley's.

'We can't find her, Roma,' Lachlan said when they called in at the store to give her the news.

'Who's this?' It was another 'mate' of Jack's, a truck driver who had pulled into town unexpectedly and was cajoling Jack into a few beers out the back once he had shut up the shop.

'Nancy Walpir,' Roma Dyer said. There were few secrets in Borragidgee.

'Nancy? Now I know Nancy, and I'll be darned if I didn't. . .yes, I'm sure it was her. Just as I was coming into town she was hitching out in the direction of Darwin. I didn't think anything of it, I'm sorry.'

'Why should you?' Lachlan said. 'It was definitely her?'

'Yes, I'm sure of it now that you've given me the name. Thought I recognised her at the time, but couldn't think just who she was.'

For the fourth time that evening Lachlan and Elspeth climbed into the high front section of the Toyota and banged the heavy, echoing metal doors. It was quite dark now. The headlights scoured the dark road beyond the town, bringing pebbles and potholes into stark relief.

The road was due for a good grading. Low shrubs loomed on either side of the drainage ditches that lined the route and insects whirred into the glare of light and spattered against the windscreen. With knees bare below her blue uniform, short sleeves, and thick hair piled on top of her head, Elspeth was chilly. She massaged the goose-pimples on her forearms and Lachlan, noticing the movement, reached forward and switched on the heater, bringing a welcome blast of warm air until the chill was gone.

They drove for ten miles but there was no sign of Nancy, and finally Lachlan slowed the vehicle, spun the wheel and turned back for Borragidgee.

'Someone's picked her up,' he said. 'She would have been hitching, not hiding. I doubt she's crouched in all that dry scrub.'

'Who in earth would be passing to pick her up?'

'This road isn't always as deserted as it looks now. Stockmen, miners. The road from the south entrance of Walkadu joins this one about five miles from town, so there are campers and tourists too, occasionally. You pick up hitch-hikers in this country, unless they look dangerous, because you know they might not get another chance of a ride for hours. She's on her way to Darwin.'

'Not Brisbane?'

'Brisbane eventually. Who knows? Whatever the case, there's nothing more we can do.' There was silence for several minutes, then he spoke again. 'I'm sorry I was angry, Ellie.'

'You were right to be. That stupid impulse to buy dessert!'

'It was an adorable impulse.'

'Just badly timed.'

'It looks as if she was determined to get away. Our medical centre isn't a prison. She would have found a way tomorrow if not today, and even if we could have kept her there by sheer force that's not the way to get through to her problems. Can we forget about it now, since there's nothing more we can do, and enjoy our evening the way we'd planned. . .cherry pie and all?'

'I can if you can.'

'Meaning, am I the sort of person who bottles up my anger and vents it all over again later? No, I'm not.'

Not *that* sort of a person, but what sort of a person? Ellie wondered as the evening passed. She found that he had set the dining-room table with china and linen and silver candlesticks holding warm orange candles. They ate only by the two circles of golden light, which reflected through the ruby pools of red wine in stemmed glasses. They talked as they had talked in Darwin, of Borragidgee and the people who had been at the wedding, of other episodes in their lives, of travel and world affairs.

Something, though, was missing, and Ellie could only conclude that there was an element of him, an inner element, that she did not yet know. That night, his touch was brief as they lay in the dark bed together, and she was asleep before it had really registered in her mind: there had been no lovemaking today.

A flock of sulphur-crested cockatoos wheeled to rest in the shaggy mane of a splay-footed old eucalypt that shaded the dry, pebbled and sandy bed of a wide creek. The sun stood high in an impossibly blue sky, and when Lachlan stopped in the shade with the picnic basket Elspeth nodded. 'Yes, the sun would be too hot, wouldn't it?' She found a patch of ground where the sand was smooth and comfortably fine, then spread the tartan picnic rug down.

'I'll make a hearth and gather a bit of wood,' Lachlan said.

He had suggested cooking a light barbecue and boiling a billy for fresh tea, rather than making do with thermos water, tea-bags and cold meats, and now she could see why. This was a delightful spot, and it would be relaxing and pleasant to loll on the rug while pale flames crackled beneath the blackened billy.

A fire was always such a companion. In the Northern Territory you never needed one to warm your house, but an outdoor picnic fire, set between big smooth river pebbles and pungently flavoured with eucalyptus smoke, was even better. Lachlan was searching for the right stones now, heaving a square, flat-topped one into the chosen spot with a pull of capable muscles and then catching sight of some more suitable candidates further afield.

'I'll find some kindling,' Elspeth offered, scrambling to her feet again after deciding that their picnic things should remain in the basket to be protected from ants and flies for as long as possible.

She walked upstream—or what she assumed to be upstream, since the creek-bed was completely dry—and scouted around the dry strips of shredded eucalyptus bark, brittle twigs and sturdier branches to go on later, returning to their picnic spot with a scratchy armful which she dumped beside the newly-laid ring of stones. Lachlan, casually dressed in denim jeans, pale rubber-soled shoes and a navy T-shirt, squatted beside the hearth.

'Found some old fencing-wire,' he said, twisting it expertly into a rough grill where their skewers of marinated chicken and lamb could rest above the coals.

'Isn't a bit dirty?'

'The flames'll sterilise it safely,' he said. 'We'll build them up at first, then let them die down to coals. Not too hungry to wait, are you?'

'Not at all, since we had that whole block of chocolate in the car. . . But you've only been in Australia for three years,' Ellie accused. 'How do you come to know so much bushman's lore? Fencing-wire grills, and so forth.'

He shrugged disarmingly. 'I like to learn new tricks,' he said. 'And I *don't* like to stick out like a sore thumb. Getting to know the bush seemed important up here.'

'You know it far better than I do,' Ellie said ruefully. 'And I've lived in Australia all my life.'

'I get the impression up here that Melbourne scarcely counts as Australia.'

'That's up here,' Elspeth retorted, loyal to the city of her birth. 'But you're right, the city is very different and my parents aren't bush people.'

'Are *you* a bush person?' he queried lightly, twisting sheets of old newspaper—cheating slightly: it should be dry leaves, he had said earlier—into tight knots and laying them in a regular grid pattern on the flat surface of sand he had carefully smoothed out within the ring of stones.

'I think so,' she answered after a pause, equally lightly. 'I think I could be. Perhaps that's what brought me to the Top End.'

It seemed odd to be playing the role of newcomer opposite a Scotsman, and the fact that he was her husband only added to the topsy-turvy sense of things. She sat on the rug and watched him quietly as he began to break up the bark and sticks she had brought and lay them tidily on top of the newspaper, keeping to the grid pattern to allow plenty of air-flow to fan the flames when the fire was lit.

He was focused on his task and his movements, made with bare, muscular forearms, broad shoulders and tanned fingers, were deft and sure. He stood after a moment and broke heavier pieces of wood into manage-able lengths by placing his foot on each angled branch and stamping down on it to create a sharp, cracking sound.

Here in the bush they were utterly alone. Behind them the crooked red cliff of a gorge towered up, higher on the far side of the creek than on this side so that from their picnic spot a sweep of undulating park-like scrub could be seen. The cliffs on the far side were cracked open at the point further upstream where this creek broke from a higher plateau and came cascading down. In a flood, or in the bottom fringe of the tropical monsoons which reached this far in a good season, the water tumbling through the rocky chasm and pooling at the bottom would be an impressive sight.

During the drive here through cattle country and the southernmost reach of the park, they had seen three tourist vehicles; but no one else had chosen this dramatic spot—marked on the map only by the dotted blue line that showed a dry water-course—for a lunch-stop or camping place. People got lost in the bush sometimes, or their cars broke down and they had to camp for days while waiting for rescue. How would it feel, Ellie wondered suddenly, to be stranded in this country with Lachlan?

With steady fingers he struck a match against the rough purple side of the matchbox, cupping it carefully with his other hand although there was almost no breeze. He put the match to the newspaper, a touch to each twisted shape, and in a few seconds flames were leaping to devour the brown and white bark which curled and glowed as it was consumed.

To be stranded in the bush with Lachlan. . . I wouldn't be afraid, Elspeth realised. I'd trust him, I'd do whatever he said, and I know we'd get safely home again.

A crow gave its mournful descending cry, climbing with a rhythmic pull of black wings up the warm air currents that rose against the rocky cliffs of the gorge. It was a lonely sight and a lonely sound but Elspeth felt no loneliness today as she had done at intervals since the wedding, and here in the bush the silence that had fallen now between herself and Lachlan didn't seem to hint at emotional distance. For today, it was a satisfying companionship.

Lachlan sat back on his heels and watched the flames, squinting against the stinging blue smoke, happy with the fire he had made. He took the rough, rusty grill and balanced it between three of the stones in his circle.

'We can't leave the fire,' he said. 'Even in the middle of a bare stony creek bed like this. You know how disastrous a bushfire can be in this country.'

'Yes, of course; but I thought the bush needed to catch fire at intervals,' Elspeth said. 'Don't some kinds of Australian seeds only germinate after intense heat?'

'There's a difference, though,' Lachlan answered,

'between deliberately or carelessly caused fires and the fires that come naturally from lightning strikes, or the fires that the Aborigines used to light to smoke out good game and promote a fresh growth of grass. An arsonist's fires are the worst, of course, because he'll make darned sure they take hold and light them in several places at once, or use petrol——'

'I've never understood how anyone could do it,' Ellie said.

'Boredom? A sense of power?' Lachlan hazarded. 'I don't understand it either. Carelessness, too, makes my blood boil. We won't go exploring that gorge till this creature's thoroughly doused. Mind a lazy hour or two?'

'Not at all,' Elspeth laughed.

She lay back on the rug, heaping the smoky green cotton pullover she had brought but didn't need into a pillow shape to place behind her head. Soon she slipped into a lazy doze, lulled by the fragile sounds of the bush all around and by the hiss and crackle of the flames. She awoke to the smell of grilling meat and saw Lachlan turning the skewers to reveal that one side of the meat was already deliciously browned.

'You're doing all the work,' Elspeth said.

'Work? This is the fun part,' he retorted. 'You can start getting out the bread and salads if you like.'

'Oh, I see! Grabbing the good job while I'm asleep and leaving me the dull one!' she teased.

Their meal was delicious as only a meal eaten out of doors could be, and then Lachlan built up the fire till it roared and heated a billy-can of water for tea, stirring the brew with the traditional eucalyptus twig.

'Ready for a hike?' he asked after the tea was just dregs in the bottom of each cup.

'Very ready.'

They doused the fire with the rest of the water from the billy, rolled the stones out of their hearth pattern, spread out the cooling coals and then covered them liberally with sand. Lachlan put a plastic bottle of drinking water into the blue day-pack along with two apples and some chocolate-chip biscuits, and slung it on to his shoulders with an expert movement.

They set off upstream along the creek bed, sinking ankle-deep sometimes into the coarse dry sand, then shaking out dusty socks and shoes as they emerged on to weathered veins of rock. A lizard scuttled away from them to hide behind the exposed root of a gum tree, and another flock of cockatoos wheeled overhead in the dry air. When they came to the place where the creek emerged from the narrow gorge that had sliced through the cliffs, there was a waterhole, a deep round pond of still water that would become stagnant and shrunken after a bad season but which was now limpid and fresh.

'If we were camped here, we could find a hide for ourselves behind some rocks and see the animals coming down to drink at sunset,' Lachlan said.

'It'd be lovely,' Elspeth said softly, imagining the rounded backs of red and grey kangaroos or rock wallabies as they bent down at the edge of the waterhole to send tiny ripples over the water with the touch of their gentle mouths. There would probably be a joey or two, since the past season had been a good one, scrabbling clumsily into and out of the pouches so that you felt sure their heavy tails and strong claws must wreak havoc with their mothers' soft fur.

They skirted the pond and began to climb the weathered rock and led up the narrow chasm. There was a dull echo as their feet struck the rust-coloured stone and occasionally a loose piece would skitter away underfoot with a light, dry sound.

'See the overhang up there?' Lachlan pointed to the left where a shadow darkened the rock to a cool brown.

'Yes, almost a cave.'

'Think you could make the climb?'

'I'm pretty sure, yes. There are plenty of flat places and shelving sections. It's a slope rather than a cliff.'

'Because I think we'll find some rock paintings up there. Mark Warren told me about them and described the location. I didn't write it down, though, so I could have got things slightly wrong.'

'Wouldn't it be on the map? Or there'd be a signpost for tourists——'

'Not in this section of the park. It's virtually undeveloped as yet. Most people take the other road in and see the attractions at the north end. There are some big sections of rock painting there, so this one wouldn't seem like anything special.'

'In a way, though,' Ellie said as they began to pick their way up the slope of solid rock, 'it doesn't matter if something isn't the biggest and best. When it's smaller and unsignposted and no one else is around you feel you've made a special discovery. If dozens of other people are there, and litter bins and trail guides and printed brochures, it sometimes feels as if what you're seeing is just another stop on the coach tour.'

He laughed. 'Spoken like a true explorer.'

A last clamber brought them up to the level of the cool space beneath the overhang, and Elspeth's illusion of solitude and discovery was spoilt a little: there was a soft-drink can lying on the ground. With a wry expression, Lachlan picked it up and put it into the side pocket of his back-pack, restoring the timelessness of the place. It *was* the spot Mark Warren had talked about.

There was a crooked band of paintings about ten feet long, some blurred by discolouring streaks of water that had dripped down through a hidden crack during heavy rains, others faded and overlapped by newer ones with bolder, cleaner lines. Powdered ochre of a dozen different shades ranging from creamy white through mustard and tan to purplish red had been used to make complex, stylised figures and shapes, with strong lines and patterns filled in by washes of colour.

'I don't know what it all means,' Elspeth said.

'Neither do I,' Lachlan confessed. 'Although I'd guess that some of the sections record hunting stories or Dreamtime myths. There's a fish, a goanna, a kangaroo. . .'

'And that's a man with a spear, isn't it?'

'Looks like it.'

'Perhaps we *do* need the printed brochure after all.'

'There must be a meaning in here if only we could read it.'

They studied the paintings in silence while Elspeth tried to picture herself as an Aboriginal woman hundreds of years ago, sheltering here after gathering food, or taking part in a ceremony that meshed in somehow with the pictures she saw in front of her. She tried to hear the booming rhythm of the didgeridoo played in the darkness around a camp fire, but the reality of the hot mid-afternoon and the caa-ca-a-a of a crow above the gorge was too strong.

She was here, now, and Lachlan was beside her. They turned away from the paintings and looked out over the chasm that cut its way further uphill to their left, gradually widening and becoming shallower as it reached the level of the plateau.

'Shall we follow this ledge along a bit and have our water and biscuits?' Lachlan said.

'Not here in the cave?'

'No. . .it's stupid, but that cola can has put me off. I'd rather find somewhere of our own.'

'OK.' Funny, but she understood what he meant.

They found a place where they could sit with their legs dangling over the ledge and took refreshing gulps of water and a crumbling chocolate-flavoured biscuit each, planning to set off back down the gorge while they ate their apples.

Elspeth was aware of Lachlan's hand resting on the rock just a few inches from her thigh, and when she finished her snack and saw that he had finished too, she thought that he would lean across to her, reach out for her and take her in his arms. She wanted his kiss, wanted the savoury human scent of him in her nostrils mingled with the balsam aroma of the shampoo he used in his hair, wanted the increasingly-familiar brush and pressure of his skin against hers.

But he made no move to touch her and so, afraid that her silence had breathed the need she felt, she spoke quickly. 'If I'd thought to bring my camera. . .'

'Hm?' It seemed his thoughts had been miles away.

'I let too much of my life go by without pictures, then I regret it later,' she explained clumsily. 'They don't replace memories, but they help them along.'

'There are our wedding pictures,' he offered absently.

'Oh, yes, that's right.' Her lame response seemed to go unnoticed.

'Jackie has a dark-room rigged up in her caravan,' he said. 'She'll probably have them developed by tomorrow night.'

'It must be a pretty big caravan.'

He shrugged off-handedly. 'It is.'

The mention of Jackie Harcourt pricked at Ellie like a tiny thorn in her finger, or like a pebble in her shoe. Actually she *had* a pebble in her shoe, she realised as they were walking back through the sandy bed of the creek again. 'Can we stop for a minute, Lachlan?'

He turned and frowned. 'What is it?'

'Just a stone in my shoe.'

While she sat on a rock, unlaced her shoe and shook out the pebble and a bit of gritty sand, he paced absently, and she wondered about what occupied his thoughts.

Had their silences today been due to his absorption in some private concern? It hadn't felt that way until that snack on the ledge of rock when she had started to wonder why he hadn't kissed her. She had felt relaxed until then, with a sense of companionship, but now there was definitely a distance.

When they reached the site of their picnic, Lachlan checked the fire once more to make sure it was really dead, but beyond this they did not linger at the spot, and he drove the forty miles to Borragidgee at a pace that sent dust boiling up in a cloud behind them and gave Elspeth several unexpected jolts. It was only as they neared the town that he spoke again.

'There's a bit of an odd job I'd like you to do tomorrow. In fact it crops up with monotonous regularity. I'll send Annie with you this first time, but later you'll be on your own.'

'What is it?' she asked reluctantly. Talking in this practical vein, he seemed to be putting a final seal of bland unimportance on the day she had earlier thought so delightful.

He made a face. 'Making sure our STD patients take their medication as prescribed. There are four in the district at the moment, and I think you'll find it takes the whole morning.'

'Surely they can. . .we could run a clinic.'

'They don't come to it. You were busy yesterday when Tim Hobbs came in and had a ceftriaxone injection. It's not the first time. He comes in with the symptoms, feeling miserable, gets the injection then acts as if the follow-up doxycycline doesn't count. You'll find out pretty soon what the attitude is like. Sorry to hit you with this, but it's one of the things that's been taking up too much of my time—my only free time in a week, often.'

'All right, of course.'

'Annie has been round with me before. I'll tell you the rest of the details in the morning and give you the list then.'

Back at Borragidgee, he disappeared into the office to do some paperwork and Elspeth showered and changed into a red jersey dress, feeling dusty and soiled from the day and needing the colourful lift of the comfortable garment. Since they had eaten a late, filling lunch, Ellie made scrambled eggs for tea, which they finished at nine.

At half-past nine, a knock at the door brought in a party of six miserable bush campers. Three of their number had come down with food-poisoning and they had hiked all day back to their two vehicles—which had no radio to call the Flying Doctor—and driven for five hours, half the time through darkness, over a winding and rocky track to emerge from the wilderness area to intersect with the road to Borragidgee about fifteen miles north-east of the town.

By the time the healthy ones had organised beds at the hotel—which rarely catered for overnight guests—and the ill ones had been put in the three-bed ward, tested for kidney function, blood-pressure and temperature and started on intravenous fluids, it was nearly midnight.

'They need to be kept under close observation, Ellie,' Lachlan said. 'I'm still doing quarter-hourly blood pressure checks on young Ross and getting fluid into him as fast as is humanly possible.' He had decided to play it safe with a wide-spectrum antibiotic as well. 'I'll make up the folding bed in the office and spend the night in here.'

Elspeth nodded tiredly, and went to bed to spend the night alone.

CHAPTER SEVEN

'ANNIE! Annie! And Elspeth!'

It was Jacqueline Harcourt running towards them across the bare, baked space of ground that served as a car park for the Cricketer's Arms Hotel, an establishment that would host cricketers only once a year following the local picnic match.

'Hello, Jackie,' Elspeth said slowly, wondering why she always got the impression that Jackie's acknowledgement of her presence was an afterthought.

'Hello, Miss Harcourt,' Annie said at the same time.

'Silly girl!' The English journalist reached out a slim hand and pushed the Aboriginal girl gently on the shoulder. Three chunky gold rings glinted on her fingers as she did so. 'You can call me Jackie too. I've told you that before. I'm glad I've caught you, though, because I wanted to ask you how your granny is. Annie is Granny Alice's granddaughter,' she explained brightly in an aside to Elspeth.

'Haven't seen her since the weekend,' Annie said.

'Oh, that's right, I forgot,' Jackie beamed. 'You live in town, don't you?'

She spoke in the exaggerated and rather self-conscious tones one might use to a particularly intelligent six-year-old, Elspeth thought, irritated. In fact, Annie was nineteen, with an intelligence and personality that were quite comfortably and pleasantly average.

'Yes, with Mr Partridge,' the Aboriginal girl nodded. Annie boarded with the schoolteacher, Jim Partridge, and his family.

Elspeth began to edge towards the medical centre's

117

Toyota, which was parked about ten yards off, and was about to make a polite farewell to Jackie Harcourt when Annie spoke again. 'We're going out to Walgunya this morning. I'll see Granny Alice then.'

'Out to Walgunya? Could I *possibly* beg a ride, Elspeth?'

'Oh. . . I——'

'Lachlan took me out there once before, and I've been with Peter Dane, of course, as you know.'

'All right, then,' Ellie nodded, trying to hide her reluctance. 'You know we'll be there only a short time, I hope, and then we'll be stopping at a couple of other places on the way back?'

'That's fine. Everything I can learn about the area and what people do, the better it is for my book. I'll bring my camera. . .if you wouldn't mind terribly stopping off at the caravan so I can pick it up. It was a piece of luck running into you today.'

'The caravan's not far, is it? I'm afraid I don't know. . .'

'Oh, no, not far at all.' Jackie climbed into the back seat, the high reach of her right leg stretching cream cotton trousers too tight over her shapely thighs.

Elspeth started the engine and Jackie directed her along a track that led from beside the tiny school to a line of trees that marked the creek. Beneath a paper-bark was parked a small Suzuki four-wheel-drive, and behind that was the long silver shape of an enormous and luxurious-looking caravan, with power cables connecting it to a petrol-driven electric generator that had been housed for protection in a makeshift galvanised iron shelter of tent-like shape. Jackie unlocked the door, emerged a moment later with her camera bag, turned back as she remembered something else, then reappeared again.

Ellie looked at her watch. Ten past ten already. She

and Annie had set off on their round at eight-thirty but had only caught up with one patient so far, a pleasant-faced Aboriginal woman with two school-age children, who had said, yes, she'd remembered to take her pills last week but hadn't been so good the last couple of days because all the symptoms seemed to have gone. She took her doxycycline under Elspeth's supervision and promised she'd remember the final three doses. She was one patient who, according to Lachlin, was unlikely to become re-infected.

Next, Annie had said, 'Try Paddy Reilly now, 'fore he goes to the pub.'

Paddy Reilly, whose first name was listed officially on his file as Marmaduke, was an ex-drover who had fetched up in his old age at Borragidgee, no one quite knew why, it was certain that his Irish parents must have had a grander destiny in mind for him when they came up with his Christian name.

'Isn't it a bit early for the pub?' Elspeth asked Annie.

She shrugged. 'They open if someone comes in, and they've got the campers there this morning.'

'That's true.' They would be there at least another night. The three victims of food-poisoning were still in need of bed-rest and professional care, the gruelling trip back from the overnight camp where the illness had struck them having compounded the initial dehydration and trauma to their systems. Lachlan would stay with them this morning until Ellie's return, then she would be left in charge while Lachlan made two routine visits.

But Paddy Reilly wasn't at home, nor was he at the hotel. He seemed to have mislaid himself somewhere between the two.

'Did you try down where he keeps his racehorse?' Margery Allyson, who owned the Cricketer's Arms with her husband, suggested.

'His *racehorse*?' Ellie exclaimed.

It didn't fit in with the idea she was forming of Paddy Reilly, but apparently the old man did have an odd-looking old mount which he was busily training for a bush race meeting later in the year, much to the town's amusement. The animal was kept in a shed-cum-stable near the poorly grassed sportsground a mile out of town on the Darwin road, but when they found the place, and the horse—which did look as if it was waiting for a visit from someone bringing food—there was no sign of Paddy.

'Surely he'll remember a simple course of pills,' Elspeth said, starting to feel a bit frustrated.

'Not him, he's the worst,' Annie said confidently. 'Says they're made of sugar. We'll have to try again after Walgunya.'

'Let's just look in at the hotel again on our way through town,' Elspeth suggested, running a finger round the inside of a uniform collar that already felt both dusty and damp.

The old man still hadn't turned up, though, and this was the point at which they had met up with Jackie Harcourt. On the journey out to Walgunya, the English journalist kept up a steady stream of questions to Annie, and Elspeth found herself trying to work out what it was all for. It definitely didn't seem just a matter of friendly chat. She was beginning to suspect that Jackie never engaged in friendly chat but always had a hidden purpose, whether journalistic or not, and wondered what the reason was for the dinner invitation she and Lachlan had accepted for tonight.

'I suppose Granny Alice has told you a lot of stories about the sacred Dreaming and the ancient lore?'

'She talks a bit. Not so much now. She's getting real old.' Annie shifted and straightened the skirt of her blue checked uniform.

'Do you like to hear about it all? Do you practise the

ceremonies?' Jackie was leaning forward from the back seat, her seatbelt unfastened, and Annie had turned a little in her own seat to look at her.

'I've got my own way of thinking about things,' she answered obliquely. 'Me and my Mum. Granny Alice knows about the land. We're Christians now, but it's the same thing, it comes down to the same, same ideas, with a lot of things.'

'You're saying you infuse the Christian rituals with ones from your own Dreaming?' Jackie asked eagerly.

Elspeth, listening quietly during all this, thought that that wasn't what the girl had meant, but in any case she seemed to have had enough of the questioning and after a non-committal shrug she turned back to look out of the passenger window and a moment later said, 'Wild pig, look, four of 'em, under that tree.'

Jackie craned her head and Elspeth risked a brief glance away from the road, but neither of them could see the animals even when Annie described their location more accurately.

At Walgunya, the work of a large cattle station was in full swing and the two uniformed medical workers were clearly thought of as an amusing sort of nuisance. Granny Alice was sitting on the veranda steps that led up to the homestead building, along with two other old Aboriginal women, one of whom was weaving a dillybag out of feathers that would be quite an art object when it was finished.

Jackie sat down and began to chat while Annie and Elspeth tried to find out from the women where they might see Jacky O'Day, the patient they had come to treat, and Bob Gunurra, who Lachlan said was worth checking on as he was a likely candidate for re-infection.

'Ask Joe down at the yards,' they were told.

Fortunately, Annie knew where the yards were. Four

men gathered round them there, greeting them above the bellow and thud of red brown beef cattle.

'Happens all the time, this medical stuff,' one of the stockmen said.

'Well, yes, it does seem to, I suppose,' Elspeth said. Jacky O'Day had also become re-infected, after earlier treatment for the same complaint had brought a cure.

'What will you give us if we tell you where Jacky and Bob are?' said another, grinning very whitely from beneath a felt bushman's hat pulled low over his brow.

'Nothing, you old devil,' Annie said loudly.

Ellie was quite surprised at the fierce tone. Clearly, this was a place where Annie felt at home. A red-eyed beast met Ellie's wary glance batefully then lifted its head to bring out a long low 'moo', as if it thought that Ellie, on the other hand, didn't fit in at all.

'Well, they're both out at Two-mile Bore,' the third stockman said, giving up the game. 'Windmill's gone crook.'

'Right-oh, Barry, thanks,' Annie said, and they walked back to the Toyota which Elspeth had driven a couple of hundred yards from the homestead at Annie's direction.

'Where's Two-mile Bore?' Ellie asked, taking the wheel again.

'Two miles from here,' Annie grinned.

'Makes sense, I suppose.' Ellie nodded coolly, then joined in the Aboriginal girl's quick giggle with a responsive laugh of her own.

They pulled up beside the bore tank ten minutes later and heard metallic banging and cheerful swearing as two men worked on fixing the broken windmill. There was an expanse of red, dusty ground surrounding the drinking trough that was fed by the tank, as well as a simple stockyard. This must be where they brought the cattle to drink when it was too dry elsewhere.

A not unpleasant animal smell lingered faintly in the air, mingled with the tang of eucalyptus, the acrid taste of dust and the mineral-filled flavour given off by the big, round tank of water. Elspeth breathed in the unique and potent blend, feeling an unexpected rush of pleasure at the fact that she was out here in this wide and earthy landscape.

The banging stopped as the two workmen realised that a car had arrived, and they came over with familiar greetings for Annie and reserved but friendly ones for Elspeth. They hadn't been among the odd assortment of wedding guests and were meeting her for the first time.

Bob admitted that he did have some symptoms again, nodding his head reluctantly at Elspeth's suggestion that he come to the clinic on Friday for an injection. Then Jacky admitted that his pills had 'gone missing' a few days ago.

'I've brought some more,' Elspeth said coolly.

Jacky gave the impression that if he agreed to be given the medication at all, it would only be as a favour to two pretty nurses, and Elspeth began to point out that, on the contrary, it was very much in *his* interest that she and Annie were going through this rigmarole; but Annie made a face halfway through the explanation and Ellie realised that it was pointless.

Instead, she simply got out the pill bottle and watched Jacky O'Day steadily as he swallowed. Doxycycline as a follow-up to ceftriaxone was a wonderful drug, but even it couldn't find its way into a patient without that patient having at least some interest in the idea. Jacky would have to be checked on again, and Ellie would have to keep track of whether Bob turned up at Friday's clinic. The men were back at their work, having pulled Annie along with them to 'take a look at what we're doing' before Elspeth had even finished noting down what she had done.

Back at the homestead, Jackie and Granny Alice seemed to have disappeared. The other two old women were inside the house helping to get some lunch for the men, so Annie and Elspeth had no choice but to sit and wait. Annie honked the horn of the Toyota energetically for half a minute as well, but there was no immediate response.

'Time? Well, God made plenty of it,' Elspeth muttered darkly to herself as she sat on the veranda steps, hoping that the skirt of her uniform wouldn't be made ruinously dust-stained as a result.

The sun was pleasant but hot on her bare legs, and her face was in the shade given by the veranda roof, which was also very pleasant. She picked up a stray stick and began scratching aimlessly in the dust with it, watching a line of ants crossing the ground on important ant business.

Time passed at a leisurely trickle. The outback attitude towards it was all very well, but Lachlan wanted her back as soon as possible, and Jackie could scarcely claim to come from a culture in which an hour or two's delay here and there was unimportant.

After about fifteen minutes, the incongruously paired women appeared together through a gap in the trees and were soon back at the veranda. Granny Alice's walk was nimble but occasionally weaving, while Jackie walked a little in front of her, clearly having to make an effort to check her excited stride to match the older woman's slower pace.

She's got something out of poor old Granny Alice, then, Elspeth thought cynically.

This became more evident as Jackie reached the veranda steps. The blonde journalist's blue eyes were glittering keenly and she had already pulled a small notebook from the back pocket of her pale trousers.

'We have to get going,' Elspeth said rather shortly,

wanting to forestall a long description of whatever it was that Granny Alice had said or shown or promised. The old woman looked tired and a little confused to see the uniformed nurses on the veranda instead of her usual companions.

'I'll take you in, Granny,' Annie said gently. 'Come on. Lucy and Trish are in the kitchen with Dorothy. You come on and help too, eh?'

A muttered reply came in Granny Alice's native tongue and Annie replied in the same language, punctuated by 'OK?' and 'all right?' They disappeared inside the house.

'Want to put your camera and bag in the car?' Ellie asked Jackie. The things looked heavy hanging around the journalist's neck and weighing in her hand, and in addition the suggestion was a way of getting Jackie into the car so that as soon as Annie came. . .

'Yes, if you could.' Jackie pulled the strap over her head and gave the whole kit—two cameras and a lens bag—to Elspeth. 'I've *got* to have a drink of water, I'm completely parched.'

She disappeared inside the house as well. Another delay. It was well after noon already and they still had Tim Hobbs to see, five miles out on a side road on the way back to Borragidgee, as well as making another attempt at finding Paddy Reilly.

Once they were finally on the move again Elspeth drove as quickly as she dared, not caring that Jackie in the back seat was bouncing over each bump so that the springs in the upholstery squeaked and wheezed loudly. Strangely, the journalist hadn't spoken about her morning with Granny Alice. She still seemed excited and was making an attempt to write notes when the road was smooth enough to permit her pen to make reasonably steady contact with the paper. Elspeth also took advantage of the smooth stretches and sped up even more.

Halfway to Tim Hobbs' turn-off, something seemed

to be going wrong with the vehicle—the steering, to be precise—and when Elspeth tried a gentle pressure on the brake before a deeper rut in the road. . .

'We'll have to stop.' Her voice came from between gritted teeth. 'I think we've got a flat tyre.'

A minute later the three women stood around the vehicle, gazing in silence at the squashed rubber of the front passenger's side wheel. Behind them, the dust in the Toyota's wake settled silently on the road. All around them, the heat pressed silently on the bush.

'Don't look at *me*,' Jackie said with a shrug and a drawl. 'I mean, the spirit is willing but the flesh is weak. I can never work out where to put the jack, or how to get the wheel nuts off.'

'Someone come along pretty soon,' Annie offered hopefully.

'We'll be long gone by then,' Elspeth answered resolutely.

With a confident appearance that masked her self-doubt, she strode to the back hatch of the vehicle and found the spare wheel, pulling it out and bracing it against her front, not worrying any more about possible marks on her uniform. The wheel wasn't new and she could only hope that it was properly inflated. Next she found a small hydraulic jack and positioned it in what she hoped was the right place on the undercarriage. There was a dimple in the metal that looked distinctly welcoming, at least.

Jackie gave an ineffectual couple of turns to the jack handle but kept pulling it out of the socket accidentally, and in the end seemed quite willing to hand it over to Elspeth, who had more success—through sheer angry willpower, she secretly thought, rather than any superior native ability.

'Car coming,' Annie announced, having delegated the role of sentinel to herself.

A sandy haired, hairy eared, rough-faced man leant on his elbow out of the driver's window and said with amused condescension, 'Need some help, girls?'

'No, we're all right, thanks,' Elspeth answered firmly, thoroughly drowning Jackie's gushing beginning of, 'Oh, that would be lovely!'

'Sure?'

'Yes, we're quite sure, thanks.'

The man roared off again, dust boiling in his wake so that it was advisable to keep one's eyes and mouth shut for a couple of minutes.

'Elspeth, was that a good idea?' Jackie drawled once the dust had cleared. 'Sending away our knight in shining armour?'

'I've done this before,' Ellie answered shortly, and with some inaccuracy. She had helped friends do it twice, both times on a much smaller car.

The wheel nuts were stiff and there was one that simply wouldn't come loose until Annie stepped in and stamped her foot down several times on the socket wrench handle, saying, 'This ought to do it.' Fortunately it did, and they used the same method for tightening the nuts firmly again when the big, heavy wheel had been manoeuvred successfully, and more easily than Ellie had feared, into place.

With fingers crossed, Ellie let down the hydraulic jack. Was the tyre properly inflated? Yes, it was, and she realised that Lachlan was too responsible to drive around the outback roads in a medical vehicle with an inadequate spare tyre.

At last they were on their way again. Half an hour later, of course, they found that Tim Hobbs was not at home. Two trucks stood in front of his ramshackle house but both were rusted hulks, and a quick tour of the yard—also filled with vehicles or pieces of them— brought forth no sign of humanity.

'We can't wait, Ellie said desperately. It was after two by this time. 'But we could leave a note.'

'Don't think he reads too good,' Annie offered.

'Is he very old, then?'

'No, he's quite a young bloke. City feller, once.'

'What on *earth* does he do out here?' Jackie squeaked. Ellie had been wondering the same thing.

'Shoots roos and rabbits. Tans hides. Fixes cars. Has a little goldmine, but don't think he's ever got much out of it.'

'Does he live alone?'

'Yeah, he does. He's a real loner, 'cept when he goes into Darwin.'

'Hm,' Jackie drawled. 'I suppose that's why he's on the Borragidgee medical centre's register of sexually transmitted diseases.' She had correctly guessed, although she had not been told, that this was what they were treating on their round today. She pulled out her notebook and began scratching quickly. 'Actually, much as I'd love to meet him—he's probably quite a character—I think I'm glad he's not here.'

'Yeah, there's no one else like him up here,' Annie nodded. 'We all like being with people. Don't reckon he likes people much.'

Elspeth put a big red ring around his name on her list and they drove off again. It would be at least three o'clock by the time she got back to the medical centre, she was thinking desperately, unable to feel Jackie's slightly appalled interest in the character of Tim Hobbs. All she could think of was that he was a name not crossed off her list.

It *was* three by the time she pulled into the driveway of the medical centre. In fact it was twenty past, but at least they had successfully chased up Paddy Reilly—in the Cricketer's Arms as expected. Jackie had asked to be dropped back at her caravan, and with so much time lost already another ten minutes didn't seem to matter much.

Lachlan opened the door to them just as Elspeth was about to lay her own hand on the handle. 'You've been an unholy age,' he said tersely, turning on his heel and walking back into the room ahead of them.

Ellie said nothing for a moment, taken aback by the angry set of his shoulders although she had expected him to be. . .if not angry, then at the very least threateningly impatient. 'We had a flat tyre,' she offered finally, 'as well as the sort of delays you warned me we would have—chasing up Paddy Reilly, for example. And Tim Hobbs wasn't anywhere to be found at all.'

'Hm,' was all he said, almost a grunt. He was bending over some papers on his desk and she couldn't see his face. 'This is a list of who I'm going to see. These are the Duncans' files, of course. Young Ross is looking good now. Kidney function and blood-pressure both back to what they should be. Annie, you can head off home now.

'OK, Doc. I'm not in till Monday now, am I?'

'That's right.'

The Aboriginal girl quickly gathered her things and left the office. Meanwhile Lachlan was still flinging instructions to Elspeth. 'Kate Dane's coming in for a pregnancy test at about five. I told her I'd be here but I won't be, now; I doubt I'll get back before six-thirty. I expect it'll be positive. She's feeling queasy and she retched at the smell of her sunblock cream this morning, she told me. Tell her I'm sorry I'm not here to do a full pelvic exam, but do what you can, answer her questions and give her those pamphlets in the top drawer of the files. Hang on, perhaps I'd better——'

'I'll find them,' Ellie said quickly.

'Leonie's going to stay over tonight with our three ward patients. She'll know how to reach us at Jackie's, but they're all doing so well now, as I said, and I don't want her to feel she isn't trusted after the Nancy episode. . .'

A minute later he was out of the door, and Jackie's influence on their late return had gone unexplained. Not that Elspeth had been planning to tell tales in any case, but she would have liked to be able to mention that the journalist had been with them if only to find out whether perhaps, for professional reasons, she should have said a firm 'no' to Jackie's request.

It was a lonely three hours at the medical centre, punctuated only by Kate Dane's happy reaction to the news of her pregnancy. The simple urine slide test had showed its result within two minutes and Kate had nodded, pink-cheeked. 'I was pretty sure.'

Elspeth took detailed information about Mrs Dane's personal and family medical history as well as any gynaecological problems she had had in the past, obtaining a healthy and promising picture. They also discussed diet, exercise, smoking and alcohol, and the mother-to-be turned out to be well-informed about the need for good health habits during pregnancy.

It was a significant contrast to Nancy Walpir's ignorance and apathy, and Ellie wondered what had become of the girl since her disappearance on Tuesday night. Lachlan had alerted medical authorities in Darwin in case the girl was admitted to hospital there through some post-partum complication. The normal uterine discharge had still been flowing and proper hygiene was important.

Finally Elspeth found the pamphlets on nutrition and pre-natal care that Lachlan had hurriedly referred to and gave them to Kate, who started reading them with interest while Elspeth dealt with a final piece of paperwork.

After Mrs Dane had gone, she made another check on the food-poisoning patients, Maggie, Geoff and Ross

Duncan, who were now well enough to be feeling a little restless and were pleased that they would be discharged in the morning.

Lachlan did not return until a quarter to seven when Leonie had already been at the centre for half an hour, ready to take up her routine duty of overnight care. It was not as responsible a task as it sounded. All medication and equipment was locked away, with the exception of the radio, and Lachlan would call in from the radio set in the Toyota once or twice during the evening to check that all was well. Roma's arrival with the evening meal provided an added safeguard.

'I haven't changed yet.' Elspeth made an unnecessary gesture to her rather tired-looking uniform. 'I didn't know what Jackie would be expecting. Jeans, or. . .'

'I like the red jersey dress you had on the other day,' Lachlan offered briefly.

They stood in the bedroom together and he was pulling through the coat-hangers in his wardrobe in search of a clean, casual shirt.

'We'll be a bit late, but I have to have a shower,' he said. 'What about you?'

'Yes, I'd like one too,' she nodded. 'It's been a dusty day. I should have slipped one in before you got back.'

'Never mind,' he answered, then suddenly the preoccupation and impatience she had sensed in him since his anger this afternoon seemed to slip away and he smiled crookedly. 'I can think of one way we could save time,' he said.

'How's that?'

'There's room in the showeer for both of us.'

Ellie laughed and blushed, then became silent as she saw him turn away to pull grey trousers from the wardrobe, his face hidden so that she could not read his feelings. Had he been serious? In a small, hesitant voice she said, 'Actually, yes, let's shower together. It would be nice.'

A few minutes later, they were standing beneath a spray of hot, tingling needles, a little cramped together, smiling wryly at one another. Without speaking, Lachlan took a cake of oval, almond-scented soap, lathered it in his large hands and began to rub it over her body till she was covered in a creamy foam that cleaned away the day's sweat and dust from back, thighs, stomach, shoulders, breasts. As she took the soap from him and began to run her hands over his own darkly thatched chest and taut back and thigh muslces, she sensed the stirring of his arousal matching her own.

When he pulled her to him with a shuddering sigh, she went willingly, slippery against him as the foamy soap glued their bodies together. His kiss tasted of the hard mineral-rich bore water that fed the shower system, less sweet than the rain-water they used for drinking but somehow pleasantly salty when mingled with the musky flavour of his lips. The water continued to cascade over them, gradually washing the soap away, as he drew forth her response.

She forgot that they were already late for Jacqueline's until he let her go gently and whispered, 'All rinsed now?'

Her answer came just as a nod and, without meeting his jewel-blue eyes with her own velvet-brown ones, she left the shower cubicle to bury her throbbing need for him in a vigorous rubbing with a big fluffy towel that left her skin fresh and dry but only tingling even more with awareness and sensuality.

Padding back to the bedroom in bare feet with the towel only loosely held around her waist, she felt cool breaths of air against her shoulders and breasts and found that her skin had tightened all over. Behind her, Lachlan switched off the shower taps and she heard the rustle of the plastic curtain as he stepped out to pick up his own thick towel.

Quickly she found a lacy black bra and pants and put them on with fingers that felt fat and clumsy in her haste. For some reason, she wanted to be safely dressed by the time he arrived in the room. Perhaps clothing provided a protection against her too-easy awareness of his physicality, as well as her own.

She had just succeeded in slipping the red jersey dress over her head and was lost within its folds when she heard him enter, and then the dress fell into place on her shoulders and around her waist so that she was confronted with the full length of his figure. The towel wrapped and tucked in at his hips emphasised the spare lines of his waist and the bold angles of his shoulders above, and the muscles in his back moved as he reached for the underclothing he had laid out on the bed.

Hastily, she slipped her bare feet into red low-heeled shoes, picked up her make-up bag and returned to the bathroom, knowing she did not have time to hide her dappling of freckles beneath creams and powders, but wanting to highlight lips, lashes and eyes, and dab on perfume in defiance of the strong aroma of the bush.

He came to hang up his towel just as she was smoothing in bright gloss to her lips. 'Ready?'

'Yes,' she said, zipping the make-up bag quickly.

It was moments like this that she found hardest; moments when he caught her at some daily feminine task that she was accustomed to performing in privacy. Yes, somehow having him see her apply her lipstick, rounding her full lower lip widely in front of the bathroom mirror, was harder, more intimate, than having his hands caress soapy lather over her body in the shower. It was odd and unsettling, and she had no idea why.

When he neither touched her nor spoke on the drive

to Jacqueline Harcourt's caravan, her uneasiness only deepened, and it didn't go away when Jackie flung open the door and drew what seemed like a very eager, hearty greeting from him.

'Thank goodness you're a bit late,' the English journalist drawled. 'I'm only just ready.'

She wore a flame-coloured blouse with a low scooped neckline of soft folds behind that revealed a perfect, evenly tanned back. Black satin trousers and high-heeled black sandals completed the outfit.

Elspeth and Lachlan were ushered into a lounge-room containing four fixed armchairs like aeroplane seats, as well as a small built-in dining-table. With darkness falling and the window open so that fresh evening air came through the tightly-fitted insect screens, it was very pleasant and not even unduly cramped. The journalist certainly knew how to make herself comfortable, even in a caravan.

Jackie poured a golden wine and set a large plate of hors d'oeuvres on the table within easy reach then sat down in the chair nearest Lachlan, kicking off her spiky sandals and curling her legs beneath her informally.

'The salad's in the fridge and the quiche is in the oven,' she said. 'Let's talk.'

She began to do just that, addressing herself mainly to Lachlan and listening with earnest attention to what he said in return so that Ellie, who wasn't in a talkative mood, became the observer, separated from the other two by the table and quickly becoming light-headed from the wine. It was only as she took her third smoked oyster on its savoury cracker that she realised that she had never fitted in lunch today.

Lachlan seemed to enjoy Jackie's company. Or at least there was something different about him when he was with her. Hard to work out just what it was. He seemed alert, lively, almost tense, and he answered each of her comments with great care and energy.

Ellie watched him. In the golden light of the rather dim electric bulbs, shaded by cream fittings and powered a little unevenly by the puttering generator outside, his hair took on richer highlights and his eyes seemed more vibrantly blue than ever, although they narrowed frequently in thought.

His hands moved vigorously in the air. 'But Jackie, you can't seriously mean to suggest that an important and very far-reaching decision like that should be. . .'

Ellie barely took in the sense of his words. She liked a serious discussion but felt out of her depth with the issues they were picking over. She was too new in the area to have an informed opinion—she would rather be silent than speak when *ill*-informed, and so, instead of joining in, she reached for another hors d'oeuvre. They were beautifully presented and utterly delicious.

Jackie refilled Lachlan's wine glass after he had drunk only an inch of it, then, a little while later, topped it up again along with Elspeth's and her own. Perhaps it was the effect of the wine, but Lachlan's Scottish accent sounded stronger tonight, with lilts and burrs and moments of richness that were pleasant and almost musical on the ear.

If only he'd talk to me more often like this, Ellie thought to herself, her inward ear filled suddenly with an impression not of heated debate but of his voice in her ear murmuring words of. . .

It hit her like the blast of an express train rocketing past a railway platform. Words of love. That was what she wanted to hear from him. Signs of love, shared moments in which each of them confessed to the strongest and most unaccountable feelings. Love. She loved him, had loved him since Darwin, and had only just realised it now, amid the swirling headiness of the wine.

All that talk of convenience and practicality, and the words she had used to herself—respect, friendship, trust—meant nothing. Or rather, they were only a fraction of the whole. It seemed impossible that she had not recognised it sooner, that she had been so completely led astray by cousin Amanda's silly, frivolous talk of The Spark, by Jane's agonised crushes and voluble adorations from afar, and by the fact that at first sight she had thought him too shy and not attractive in what she now knew was a meaningless movie-star image of good looks.

Those things weren't love. This was—this need for a complete and total relationship with Lachlan, not just the bland chat of friends and not just the wordless passion and shared sensuality of lovemaking in the dark, but everything in between. This was why she had felt so lost and alone when he was away on call, and why the time they had spent together had lacked an ultimate richness that she had been grasping after without understanding. It was love she wanted from him, nothing else, and as she watched him sipping his wine and talking to Jackie, who was standing at the stove, she knew that his love was what she did not have.

'Could you pop this on the table for me?' The words were a blur in the background, and Jackie had to repeat them. She was holding out a salad bowl and a long, foil-covered loaf of garlic and herb bread, and Elspeth finally realised what was wanted.

'Are you all right, Ellie?' she heard Lachlan ask. 'You've been very quiet tonight.'

His voice seemed to come from a long way away. Jackie sank a knife into the plump filling and brittle crust of a mushroom and spinach quiche, and slid a plastic serving trowel beneath a generous triangle, but the deliciously savoury aroma of cheese and egg and vegetable was blunted in Elspeth's nostrils.

'I'm fine,' she managed at last. 'I . . . I forgot to have lunch. But I'm fine.'

CHAPTER EIGHT

'THERE'S a bush dance at Nagadi on Saturday night, if you'd like to go to it,' Lachlan said, lifting his eyes from a newspaper at breakfast to meet Elspeth's gaze as he made the suggestion.

'That sounds nice.' She nodded, her words matching his everyday tone.

'And we're invited to an early barbecue dinner there beforehand. Peter thought you might be interested in a tour of the property as well, so he's suggested we go out there straight after lunch.'

'Should we bring a contribution to the barbecue?'

'That's a nice idea. A couple of salads, perhaps, and a bottle of wine.'

It was four weeks since their dinner at Jackie Harcourt's caravan, and that night's revelation of Ellie's love for Lachlan had not faded and turned false. In fact the knowledge only grew stronger and more painful within her each day till at moments like this, as she sat calmly across from him as they ate cereal and toast, it threatened to explode from her, shattering the façade of their bland conversation.

Why was it painful? Easy to answer: because Lachlan didn't love her in return. Oh, he liked her, respected her, responded to her physically. Apart from the sensual strength of their relationship, the marriage was much as she had imagined it would be when thinking about it in Melbourne—shared work which they both enjoyed, a polite respectful awareness of each other's needs in free time, the occasional outing together to a bush-walking trail or picnic spot.

137

And yet it was all so inadequate, like a soup made without stock, or a mouthful of tap-water when you yearned for champagne. Now she was beginning to have a new fear, too: that the love she felt but could not dare to show would poison the good moments between them. Lachlan liked to sit amid his potted plants on the veranda absorbed in reading, and reading was always a pleasure that Elspeth had delighted in too; but these days the print turned to blurred black insects on the paper and she could only hear the silence between the two of them as Lachlan turned his pages; a thick silence that sounded the death knell of her peace of mind.

Last night in bed, as well, when his hands and lips had moved on her body and she had wanted to moan aloud with pleasure, she had stiffened and stifled the sounds, terrified of what she might betray in the abandonment of her release. For the first time their love-making had petered out without consummation, and she knew he was confused and frustrated about the fact.

'What is it, Ellie?' he had whispered. 'Talk to me about it.'

'No, it's nothing. I have a bit of a headache, that's all. Too much sun this afternoon.'

'Would you like some aspirin?'

'No, I'll get a drink of water and it'll go away while I sleep.'

She had scrambled from the bed and slipped into her kimono, its silk chilly at first against her hot skin and its sash somewhere on the floor where she couldn't find it in the dark, so that she had had to hug the garment to her. Returning to the bed with a full glass in her hand, she had lost her grip on the silky robe and it had fallen open. She had seen his eyes linger briefly on the full curves and planes of her figure as she had bent down to place the water on the small bedside-table, then he had rolled over roughly, making the springs of the bed creak, and had lain with his back to her.

She had sat up in bed, still wearing the kimono as she sipped the water—which she hadn't really wanted—and then slid beneath the covers. His breathing had been even and deep, but was he asleep or only pretending? It was the first time she had not slept naked beside her, although by morning the open-fronted robe had twisted around her, giving her little protection.

It was clinic day today so they were both dressed for work and had little time to linger over breakfast. Elspeth got up quickly as soon as she had downed the last mouthful of her freshly brewed coffee and began to clear up cereal packets, marmalade jars and dirty dishes while Lachlan shaved and went to open up the medical centre.

They had a quiet morning seeing a couple of local school-children and three men from the mines, as well as Kate Dane for her second pre-natal check-up. Elspeth tested her urine for glucose and albumin and took her weight and blood pressure while Lachlan questioned her about her symptoms and feelings. She had gained no weight and was beginning to suffer from unpredictable food cravings and appetite loss, but all this was quite normal and nothing to worry about so early on. Fatigue was a problem, too.

'I just can't get through the day without a long nap after lunch,' she confessed. 'It's wreaking havoc with all my chores, but John is being very good. And so is Peter, for that matter.'

'You sound surprised,' Lachlan laughed.

'Well, he's a bachelor. Aren't they notoriously put off by dreary old pregnant women?'

'No doubt some of them are, yes,' he admitted.

'I envy you when your turn comes——' Kate turned to Elspeth '—with your own training and an expert on hand to answer any questions you can't answer yourself.'

She left the medical centre and Elspeth sat at her desk, hot and confused. Thank goodness Lachlan had retreated into his office with the door closed!

'When your turn comes,' she murmured to herself. It was something she hadn't considered. Theirs being, supposedly, a practical marriage, they had been practical about the issue of pregnancy, but Kate's words made her realise just how little she had thought to look into the future. Eventually, even if they chose to wait for several years, most couples had children.

Elspeth would be thirty-one this year. Pressing her face into hands that shook a little, she realised that in her heart of hearts she didn't believe that her marriage to Lachlan would last long enough to produce children. It would end somehow, bitterly, killed off by the imbalance between them, by the painful secret of her love. She had been a fool to think that it could work, to think that a commitment such as marriage could rest only on the foundations of convenience and respect.

One proud, reckless part of herself told her to get out now, to really confirm her own growing conviction about herself, which was that she ran away whenever something got difficult. Why not go back to Melbourne and punish herself with her mother's 'I told you so', and with listening to cousin Amanda again talking about The Spark?

Another part of herself—and she honestly didn't know if it was weakness or strength—insisted that it wasn't possible to leave, that life without Lachlan so soon after she had begun to discover the depth of her feelings for him would be too hard and lonely to bear.

There came the sound of the front door opening and she lifted her head to see Florence enter. Summoning all her reserves to present a front of normality, Elspeth asked, 'How was your morning, Florence?'

'Pretty good. New family at the end of town there got some problems.'

'Have they?'

'Yes, place not too clean. Little boy got trachoma, I'd say, and his brother's going the same way, most like it. I told them to come in this afternoon, but don't know if they will. Is. . .?'

'Yes, he's in his office. No patient with him. I'm sure you can go in,' Elspeth said.

Florence gave a soft knock and disappeared into the office, leaving the door ajar. Ellie could hear her repeating the story of the new family to Lachlan, as well as giving an account of what else she had done that morning during her regular visits to some of Borragidgee's poorer homes. Able to enter such places without seeming like a busybody or a threat, she gave advice on hygiene and general health and could dispense some simple medications for such complaints as mild childhood diarrhoea, always alert, however, for things that required a doctor's or trained nurse's attention.

Elspeth looked at her watch and found that it was lunchtime. With no patients in the ward at the moment and no one waiting to see the doctor, she could safely leave the office and go into the kitchen. There, dulling her too-active mind with the routine task, she prepared ham, mustard and salad sandwiches for herself and Lachlan as well as for Florence, took out some home-made oatmeal and coconut biscuits and brought everything back into the medical centre, where she put on the kettle for tea as well.

It was just as the three of them were finishing the simple lunch that an Aboriginal woman came in with her two boys, looking a little fearful but determined. It was the family Florence had talked about and they had come earlier than expected. One child was only about two and the other looked to be seven or eight. Both children had the tell-tale symptoms of trachoma—swollen, weeping eyes with lids that were almost glued together with crusted residue.

Trachoma was the leading cause of preventable blindness in the world, Elspeth knew, and tragically it was still very common among the Aboriginal population in Australia. A severe and chronic form of conjunctivitis, it was spread by the flies which were so numerous in many outback areas—too numerous even to be waved away from their faces by small outback-bred children who became used to the unpleasant feeling of the insects crawling around their eyes, with tragic results.

Florence stepped forward and gently took the eight-year-old's fist away from his face. He had been rubbing at the painful, itching rims of his eyes. 'Show the doctor, Andy,' she said.

The boy stood stock-still while Lachlan squatted in front of him. One eyelid was inverted and it looked a mess. Lachlan wasn't long in reaching his diagnosis and decision. 'Have you ever been on an aeroplane?' he asked the boy. A big-eyed and silent shake of the head came in reply. Lachlan stood up. 'Mrs. . .' He hesitated.

Florence filled in quickly. 'Namadja.' The name sounded familiar to Elspeth but for the moment she couldn't think why.

'Mrs Namadja, we're going to send Andy to Darwin tomorrow, if we can. If not, then early next week. He'll only be gone for the day. The Flying Doctor Service will take him in their plane and he'll have a very small, easy operation which will fix that eyelid. Does that sound like a good idea to you?'

'Yes, Doctor,' she nodded. 'His eyes been sore for a long time now.'

'You didn't think of seeing a doctor before?'

'We've been at Parrawilga.' This was an isolated settlement further out west. 'No doctor there.'

'But there's the Flying Doctor out there, isn't there?'

'They gave us some ointment a couple of years ago, but sore eyes just came back. Lots of kids got it. I was busy with this one——' she touched the two-year-old on the shoulder '—and didn't have a husband after Billy died.'

'No, we're not angry with you, Mrs Namadja, don't get the wrong idea; we just want to find out what's been happening. Will you be staying to live in Borragidgee now?'

'Maybe go out and live at Walgunya. Bill Namadja, he's my boys' grandad, he's out there.'

Now Elspeth knew where she had heard the name Namadja. Uncle Bill, with his cataracts and love of chocolate biscuits must be this woman's father-in-law.

'Well, we visit Walgunya as well, and people come here from there, so I'm going to give you that same ointment again for both the boys, and this time we'll look very carefully to make sure the eye disease doesn't come back.'

He gave the woman a tube of erythromycin ointment as well as detailed instructions for its use and then sent Florence home with the family so that she could give the desert-bred mother some suggestions about how better hygiene could also help prevent the sore eyes from returning.

'You see, Ellie,' Lachlan said, pacing the office restlessly when they had gone, 'it's not just the flies, it's general living conditions, and when people don't have flushing toilets and running water, how can they keep towels clean and wash their hands regularly? According to Jackie it's all part of an iniquitous political plot to keep the indigenous people at the bottom of the heap, but that's far too simplistic.'

'What *is* the answer, then?' Ellie asked quietly, noting

the impatience with which he had tossed out the journalist's name.

'Nobody knows.' He spread his hands helplessly. 'I think that's the truth. Nobody knows. It'll take time, that's all, and meanwhile we do what we can and small advances get made. Walgunya is going well. . .'

'Funny that both Bill Namadja and his grandson have eye trouble.' It was just an idle comment and Lachlan caught her by surprise when he wheeled round to face her and grabbed her tightly by the shoulders.

'Ellie, I think you've really hit on something there. I really do!'

'What? What have I said?'

'The way to get Uncle Bill to go to Darwin for his cataract surgery. If I can arrange both operations for Monday. . . Andy's is very simple. We could have done it here if we'd had to, but I thought we'd play it safe and use Darwin just in case of complications. . .and I'll go to Walgunya tomorrow to talk to Bill, tell him the boy is nervous about the operation. I'm *sure* he'll agree to it. You don't know it, Ellie—you should, but you don't— but you're brilliant!'

He picked her up and whirled her in his arms around the room so that her head began to spin and she felt light and breathless from laughter. 'Put me down, Lachlan, I'm too heavy for you!'

'You're not, you're light as a feather.'

'Me? With my hefty bones?'

He set her down and kissed her lightly on the lips. 'With your good healthy frame, and your beautiful——' He broke off. The door had opened and Jackie Harcourt was there, a little smile playing around her lips as if there was something very amusing about the sight of them together like this. For Ellie, such frivolous moments were far too rare.

'Don't mind me,' Jackie said with a metallic laugh.

'I've just come for my repeat on the dermatitis cream. I've been squeezing this last tube dry for the last couple of days and my feet are getting worse.'

In spite of her mostly flawless skin, Jackie suffered from severe dryness and cracking around the toes and soles of her feet if she wasn't careful. It was exacerbated by the mineral content of the water at Borragidgee and she had tried several different prescription creams in her four months in the town.

'Can you get the cream for her, Ellie?' Lachlan said. 'I'd like to radio Darwin Hospital and the RFDS, then I'll call Walgunya on the open radio session this afternoon and see if I can go out there tomorrow.'

'Out to Walgunya?' Jackie was immediately alert, Elspeth could hear as she went into the small dispensary room to find the right ointment.

'Yes.' Lachlan didn't elaborate.

'Would I be able to come?' Jackie said. 'They're not too keen on me just turning up without an escort, so to speak.'

Lachlan took his hands from the radio controls and turned to face her. 'Frankly, Jackie, I'm not that keen on it either, whether you've got an escort or not. The Walgunya people like to be left pretty much alone unless there's a good reason for the visit. No one without my permit for this area is allowed out there at all. You hitched a ride with Elspeth and Annie that time. Surely you've seen enough.' He had found out about the visit through a casual phrase of Jackie's that same night in her caravan over dinner. 'What's the attraction?'

'Oh, come on, Lachlan! My research, of course. I thought you were in favour of this book. You set out to help me in the beginning.'

'And I'm still helping. I just think that the time you've spent with Alice Tirltirra, for example, is inappropriate.'

'Inappropriate!' she mimicked. 'She's been one of my most valuable contacts!'

'Well, I haven't got time to argue that out now,' he shrugged. 'Have you found the ointment, Elspeth?'

'Yes. I've got it here,' Ellie said, coming out of the dispensary room. 'Do you want it wrapped, Jackie?'

'No, don't bother, thanks.'

'. . . So I'm afraid the answer is, no, you can't come with me tomorrow,' Lachlan said firmly. 'I don't even know if I'll be going yet, till I check that it's all right.'

'In that case, I'll see you when I see you,' Jackie shrugged. 'Probably at Nagadi on Saturday night for the dance.'

She left, slipping the tube of dermatitis cream into the big leather shoulder bag she carried. Lachlan returned to the radio and reached both Darwin Hospital and the RFDS with no trouble, arranging Bill's and Andy's surgery for Monday morning, although the former operation would need to be confirmed after he had talked to the tribal elder tomorrow.

Elspeth wondered about the rather hostile exchange with Jackie. It wasn't his usual style when talking with the journalist. Did it mean he was starting to see her negative side at last? That suggested he was a poor judge of character, which didn't seem to fit with the rest of the man as she now knew him. It was a puzzle, the whole thing, and a part of her sent out a warning message: don't even try to solve it.

Lachlan's trip out to Walgunya the following afternoon was successful and he came back from it very pleased, at just after five o'clock. 'He's agreed to the surgery. Apparently he had a niece who went blind years ago. He never knew why at the time, and she's dead now, but he now realises it must have been trachoma and he's very anxious to help young Andy.'

'Are they very close?'

'No-o. Not in a Western sense, anyway. His son had drifted off before marrying Gloria, and the family only came back here once before Billy's death—when Andy was three, apparently. But now Gloria has decided to renew contact by settling in this area, and the kinship bond runs deep. Bill's also a leading tribal elder and has a very strong sense of his responsibility to the younger generation. It's mainly the middle generation that has been decimated by their sense of rootlessness and the alcoholism that followed from that, and Bill is fighting to have the next one grow up strong and proud and capable. That's partly why I was so dismayed to see the effect of those cataracts on his independence a few weeks ago.'

Elspeth nodded in silence. He really cared about what he could do here. If she had not realised it back in Darwin, she would definitely have realised it today. As they tidied the place, locked up and went through into the house, the love she felt for him burned and ached inside her like a hot, heavy stone.

He was Scottish by birth and upbringing. He had spent two years in Bangladesh and had been in Australia for three. It was probable that he would want to move on again, to some other part of the world where he felt he was needed, or perhaps to a more settled life in the city somewhere, or a provincial town. A doctor could find meaningful work almost anywhere. She wanted to go with him, wherever he went, but would their strange marriage survive?

'There's always divorce,' he had said. Did that form a part of his philosophy? Would he need to be free of ties next time he moved on? There was so much about him that she didn't yet know or understand, and the love she felt was only binding her, stopping her from finding out what she needed to know. Aware of the wide, yawning gap between their feelings, she was too afraid to probe him in the way that lovers did: 'Tell me about the time when you. . .' 'What did you really feel when you. . .?' 'What do you think you'll do if. . .?'

Perhaps it wasn't that she was afraid to ask the questions. It was hearing the answers that frightened her.

'There's a movie on tonight,' he said that evening as they prepared spaghetti and salad together for their meal. 'In the community hall at eight o'clock. Would you like to go?'

'Sounds nice.' She nodded. 'What is it?'

He named a quirky American comedy hit that had probably disappeared from city cinemas months ago, but Elspeth had missed the film in Darwin so its tardy arrival in Borragidgee did not matter. Later she found that most of the town had turned up to the makeshift cinema, as films only came to Borragidgee once a month. Jackie Harcourt was one of the few people who *wasn't* there.

In the darkness in front of them, Ellie saw a young couple snuggled closely together as they watched the film, ignoring the upright hardness of the chairs which lacked the cosiness of city cinema seats. She and Lachlan, on the other hand, did not touch. She heard his laugh beside her and tried to concentrate thoroughly on the film herself, but the need she felt for the reassurance of his arm around her shoulders or his hand reaching for hers across the small space between them went unsatisfied as it did that night when a different, thicker darkness surrounded them in the solitude of their shared bed.

No unexpected calls disturbed their free time the next morning, and soon after lunch they set off for Nagadi. Elspeth wore a full skirt of floral cotton, and a round-necked cream blouse, sturdy sandals and a wide-brimmed straw hat. The dry season was at its height now and although further south the months of June, July and August were wintry ones, here in the north the word 'winter' had no meaning. The days were hot and bright and there was little change in the time the sun set and rose between these months and those on the opposite side of the calendar.

Peter Dane greeted them cheerfully at Nagadi, reaching out a blunt, work-hardened hand to Lachlan and giving Elspeth a quick squeeze on her upper arm.

'Good timing!' he said. 'I've just finished unloading some fuel drums into the storage shed and I'm ready for a break. John and Kate are busy clearing out the big outhouse for the dance.'

'Perhaps we should help,' Elspeth suggested.

'No, they're nearly finished, then Kate'll take her nap and John'll get the barbecue fire ready.'

'We brought some salads,' Lachlan said. 'They should go in the fridge before we set off.'

'Wait here in the shade and I'll run them in,' Peter said, taking the two red plastic bowls from Lachlan's hands when the latter had retrieved them from the back of the Toyota.

Elspeth sat between the two men in the front of Nagadi's newest four-wheel-drive. It was a bouncy, bumpy, dusty ride and she was thrown against Lachlan's firm shoulder more than once. Finally he put an arm out and gripped her across the back and around her waist. 'That's better,' he said.

It was what she had been hoping he would do last night during the film for romantic reasons. Now he *was* doing it, but purely for practical ones. Pointless to let her afternoon be ruined by such a small thing! Carefully she concentrated on what Peter Dane was saying.

'We're running about nine thousand head of cattle at the moment, and that's really all we do. Kate's doing very well with her vegetables and chickens and she's even hoping to try a few tropical fruits soon, but that's all for our own consumption. The eggs we get are beaut.

I'll show you the fowl run when we get back, Elspeth. Nothing like city eggs; they've got orange yolks and are full of flavour. These are the main stockyards but we have some rougher ones further out bush if we need to take in part of the herd for any reason. . .'

They saw the property's water-hole where a lone pelican floated with silent grace, and almost disturbed a group of kangaroos lying in the shade beneath some trees on their way back to the homestead. The stock were almost all ranging freely at the moment, and there was just one herd penned into the large and well-grassed home paddock, ready for transporting south to market in a few days' time.

Nearer the homestead, Kate's efficient rows of vegetables were an impressive sight, and in a well-wired-in run nearby a dozen hens scratched in the dirt and gobbled at grain and household left-overs.

'Ready for a cool drink?' Peter said when the tour was over.

'Yes, please!' Ellie exclaimed. 'I've never appreciated cool liquids as much as I do up here.'

'Only lemon cordial, I'm afraid. Home-made. We're saving the hard stuff for later.'

'Suits us, I think,' Lachlan put in.

'Yes, I've never been quite sure what or where the yard-arm was,' Elspeth said, 'but I don't think the sun's over mine yet—or past it, or under it, or wherever it's supposed to be.'

The two men laughed and they all trooped into the house to sit in the welcome coolness and dim light of the lounge-room. Kate Dane emerged as they were finishing their drinks, her cheeks flushed a little from her recent nap, then Jim Partridge, the schoolteacher, and his family arrived, and everyone decamped to the shaded area of garden where John was at work over an open barbecue fire.

They ate as the sun slipped down behind the slim-trunked trees to the west, joined just beforehand by the enterprising trio of mine workers from the Radnor headquarters who had formed themselves into a bush band six months before. As barbecue things were cleared away and last drinks were finished, local people began to arrive for the dance, soon filling the yard in front of the homestead with more vehicles than had been there on the night of Lachlan and Elspeth's wedding five weeks ago.

Jackie Harcourt was one of the first to arrive, and graciously accepted a glass of wine, while the three band members went to set up their equipment and the others sat on in the perfect evening air around the dying coals of the fire. It seemed odd that she hadn't been invited to the barbecue, but if she resented it she did not let it show.

Ellie wondered at the omission and began to realise that, in spite of the impression Jackie gave of being a sharp observer at the centre of town life, she wasn't entirely popular at Borragidgee. Understandable, if you thought about it. Although she went through the motions of warmth and friendliness, the journalist's presence in the town was really only about one thing—getting material for her book—and perhaps it was starting to filter through to people that the book *wasn't* intended to be a series of dramatic desert photographs linked by a gushing commentary but a sizzling exposé of conflict and crisis, like the 'unauthorised biography' of some Hollywood star.

To Jackie, everyone was fair game, and perhaps it wasn't only Ellie who didn't like the idea of her marriage, her attitudes and her work being described in a way that fitted only the sensational picture Jackie wanted to create.

Lachlan gave her his usual hearty greeting, however.

Perhaps, though, it was a little forced. Elspeth thought back on the night they had eaten the delicious quiche at Jackie's caravan. Late in the evening, when he had been speaking about his years of medical training, first in Edinburgh and later in London, they had discovered the delightful coincidence of mutual friends.

He had laughed. 'Well, they say it's a small world, but this is ridiculous.'

And Jackie had returned with an animated, 'I *must* remember to mention it next time I see them. I'll be in touch with them almost as soon as I get back, which should only be a couple more months now.'

And that was a month ago. Would the journalist really be leaving Borragidgee in four weeks? Elspeth suddenly found that she was longing for it to happen.

The conversation between Kate Dane and Cathy Partridge filtered into her awareness at that point:

'. . . Oh, John and I were at daggers drawn when we first met. We couldn't agree on anything. The way he rubbished my opinions! And yet I couldn't help noticing that he always seemed to want to hear more of them. His eyes used to light up when I came into the room, he'd head straight for me, greet me like a long-lost uncle and we'd be having a raging political argument within two minutes!'

The words seemed to slot into place like a difficult section of jigsaw puzzle, making sense out of what had seemed a few moments ago like a jumble of untidy patterns and shapes.

Could it be true? Lachlan was in love with Jackie. That cheerful, hearty manner when he greeted her, the heated discussion they had had in her caravan that night about the themes of Jackie's book, the way he often spoke her name afterwards with a frown, as if she was a problem. Of course she was a problem. Another woman *was* a problem when you were in love with her and not with the wife you'd so recently married for different and much more practical reasons.

Ellie's ears burned as she listened to Lachlan and Jackie talking right at that moment. He was beside his wife, as was conventional, with Jackie on his right, while Kate and Cathy sat on Ellie's left, their words sinking into unimportance now.

'But Jackie,' Lachlan was saying with terse impatience, 'what good can that kind of sweeping analysis possibly do?'

'What good? Isn't it obvious?'

'Sweeping and inaccurate, I should have said.'

It was just the sizzling sort of debate that Kate Dane had been describing only moments ago, the kind of argument that could, between a man and a woman, become charged with the tension of desire and awareness.

Behind her, beyond the homestead, Elspeth heard the bush band tune up and begin to play, launching into a rollicking Irish melody that soon had the wooden floor of the big, open outhouse shaking and thumping with energetic feet. The ring of guests around the fire was beginning to make a move to join the dancers, and miserably Elspeth followed them, thankful for the darkness which had fallen now.

It didn't seem likely that Lachlan would notice that anything was wrong. At this sort of dance, you had no time for cheek-to-cheek or romantic eye-gazing, and you changed partners at every round of the melody. In any case, he was still talking to Jackie.

CHAPTER NINE

IT WAS starting to seem as if the dance would never end. Out in the bush where there were no movies, discos, restaurants and theatres to choose between every night of the week, an event like this one was a joyous release for the whole community, and some people had driven over a hundred miles to attend it. Since there were no neighbours to complain about noise as it grew late, the band played on and on with only brief breaks for refreshment, and Ellie was sure it must be well after midnight, although she wasn't wearing a watch.

Opposite her, a lad of about twenty jigged and smiled sheepishly, aware of his own clumsiness, then moved on to his new partner as the band swooped back to the beginning of the refrain.

'Fancy meeting you here!' Her new partner was Lachlan, and he grinned at her as he seized her hands.

They galloped down the row of dancers, split up, came together again and spun around each other. Out of the corner of her eye Ellie saw Jackie standing aloof from the dance and leaning one elbow against the rough wall of the outhouse. She wore a crooked smile and her eyes moved around the dance floor with lazy interest as if all this energetic bush-dancing was very quaint. No doubt it was. She wore the black satin pants and high sandals she had chosen on the night of the dinner in her caravan, but tonight she had topped them with a draped gold blouse which, along with the huge matching hooped earrings, looked like an outfit designed for a London disco.

Elspeth, in her wide floral cotton skirt and plain

blouse, felt unglamorous by contrast, although many other dancers were dressed as simply as she was. In fact, Jackie hadn't actually danced much. She probably couldn't gallop through Strip-the-Willow on the uneven planks of the floor in stiletto heels.

In the middle of these possibly ungenerous thoughts, Elspeth realised that Lachlan was pulling her out of the spin of the dance. 'Why. . .we haven't finished yet. What's the matter?' she stammered, confused.

'That's what I was going to ask you,' Lachlan responded. 'You don't look as if you're enjoying it any more.'

'Don't I?' Unconsciously she must have been letting her façade of gaiety slip.

'Ready to go home?'

'Well, it must be getting rather late,' she said in sensible tones. 'I'm sure they'll be stopping soon anyway, won't they?'

'Late? It's only ten o'clock.'

'Oh. Well in that case I must be more tired than I thought,' she improvised quickly. 'Of course if you want to stay on, I can easily sit out a few dances——'

'Nonsense. I've had enough. Let's go.'

He pulled her by the hand to the other side of the room where Kate Dane was sitting out a dance and they gave their thanks and goodbyes, having to raise their voices against the noise of the band.

'Elspeth's feeling tired,' he said when Kate protested at their early departure.

'Oh. . . Is she?' The mother-to-be's glance at Elspeth was suddenly curious.

She's wondering if I'm pregnant too, Ellie realised miserably.

But they were making their way out of the building before Kate could probe any further. Elspeth wondered if Jackie had noticed their departure. Lachlan hadn't seemed interested in saying goodbye to her.

Interesting, though, that when they slowed and turned into the medical centre's driveway half an hour later, the headlights which had caught up with them a few miles back swished past and could be seen to belong to Jackie's small vehicle.

On Monday morning Lachlan went out to the airstrip to meet the Flying Doctor plane and make sure that Andy and Bill Namadja were ready for their trip to Darwin and feeling good about the imminent surgery.

'I've described the two alternatives to Bill in detail,' he had reported to Elspeth earlier. 'Eye surgery is difficult psychologically under local anaesthetic. I told him exactly what it would be like from his perspective, and he knows a general anaesthetic would be easier in that sense. Of course I also explained that a general has other risks for a man his age, but his physical condition is good so really that risk is small.'

'What did he decide on?'

'The local. Now that he's determined to go through with it he wants to show his courage and firmness, particularly when I explained that Andy's operation would definitely be done under local.'

'They'll only do one of Bill's eyes today though, won't they?'

'Yes, and the other one in about six months' time if he's in favour of it. I think he will be. They're also planning to insert an artificial lens. He'll have the vision of a thirty-year-old man once the dressing comes off, and I think he'll be over the moon.'

So Elspeth opened the medical centre alone. It wasn't an official clinic day but the RFDS often had a message to convey over the morning radio session and Lachlan liked to make sure everything was in readiness in case of an emergency. Next week there was a round of immunisations scheduled, and this would keep Elspeth busy for at least two days.

The regular morning radio hook-up between people all over this area of the outback, often called the 'galah' session after a noisy Australian bird, passed with no messages for the Borragidgee Medical Centre. Elspeth left the equipment—which seemed familiar now in spite of its initial strangeness—set up to receive incoming emergency calls.

She was about to start planning her immunisation route with the aid of a map, some instructions from Lachlan and a list of names and places, when she heard what sounded like someone outside. She put down the map and listened. Was it Lachlan? She hadn't heard the Toyota, nor his quick, confident feet on the cement path and up the wooden steps. In any case, it was too early for him to be back. Perhaps it was no one after all.

The sound came again—a creak and a shuffle, as if someone was standing just outside. Or was it simply a stray dog investigating an unexplainable scent? If it *was* a dog, it ought to be shooed away. It wasn't easy to keep a medical centre clean and germ-free here in the outback, and the last thing they needed was an encampment of dogs or cats in the space between floor and earth. A wooden lattice-work supposedly prevented anything from entering the space, but perhaps it had come loose at some point. Elspeth got up and went to check, opening the door and looking down with a doggish scold readied in her voice.

But it wasn't a dog. It was Nancy Walpir. She must have been standing on the lower step for several minutes making up her mind to knock, and when she saw Elspeth, who quickly dropped her dog-scolding expression, she stepped back nervously.

'Hello, Nancy,' Elspeth said with careful but not overpowering friendliness.

'I want to come to hospital again,' came the blurted reply.

Ellie didn't quite know what to do and was desperate for Lachlan's return. The girl looked thin, unhealthy and not very clean, but did she really require bed-rest and hospital care? It was sheer procrastination that led Ellie to suggest a shower, clean clothes and a cup of tea to start with, but it seemed to be the right thing. Nancy relaxed noticeably, as if she had been afraid before that her return to the medical centre would begin with some kind of punishing medical treatment.

'Can you manage the shower by yourself?'

'I got a few sores. They sting, some of 'em, if they get wet.'

'Sores?'

'Just cuts or bites, they started out. Then you scratch them. . . Don't seem to want to get better.'

'Perhaps I'd better have a look.'

Nancy took off a pair of tattered green synthetic trousers and rolled up the sleeves of an old workman's shirt to show several sores that were either weeping or infected, and had been clearly far too slow to heal, giving an indication that she had been eating very poorly and living in dirty conditions. Ellie explained that they should be gently washed in the shower even if they did sting, and afterwards she would treat them properly with antiseptic, ointment and dressings. Nancy disappeared into the shower-room.

Not wanting to risk insulting the girl by actually consigning the dreadful clothes to the garbage can, Ellie put them in a plastic bag planning to wash them later on. In the store-room there was a small assortment of very cheap but new clothes for just this sort of occasion, and Elspeth found pink cotton underwear and a simple short-sleeved dress in a pattern of irregular cream and beige stripes.

She had made a pot of tea and found some sweet biscuits when Nancy emerged from the shower-room dressed in fresh garments, but decided to take a routine check of temperature, blood pressure and pulse before they each sat down to the hot drink. The open sores should be dealt with too.

Nancy seemed relieved to be receiving the treatment. She sat quietly while Elspeth cleaned the worst of the sores using tweezers to pick out some grains of dirt that hadn't been washed off in the shower. Then Ellie sprinkled each area of broken skin with antiseptic powder and used a soothing cream on some chafed areas as well.

It was as she fixed the final dressing into place that she heard the Toyota outside. Giving way to her first thoughtless impulse, she jumped to her feet and was about to rush outside to tell Lachlan of Nancy's return, but the quick return of common sense told her that this would only make the girl self-conscious and convince her that she was being discussed out of earshot. Improvising, Elspeth went to the kitchen and put more water in the electric kettle to boil.

'That's Lachlan,' she said. 'I'm sure he'll want tea, too. Are you ready for yours?'

Nancy nodded, and so when Lachlan entered the medical centre, there she was, calmly crunching on a ginger-nut biscuit and blowing on the top of her tea to make it cool, while Elspeth topped up the teapot in the kitchen.

'Nancy!'

'She's asked if she can come back into our ward,' Elspeth said quickly, thrusting a steaming mug into his hand.

He sat down. 'That should be possible. . . You've hurt yourself, Nancy?'

'Just sores that won't get better. She's cleaned them up for me now.'

'That's good,' he nodded, studying her and taking a biscuit from the plate Ellie held out. 'I'll give you some pills to take for them as well. . . A course of erythromycin, Ellie. . . What's been happening to you, Nancy?'

'Oh. . .' she shrugged '. . . I was no good. I was real stupid.'

'Well, it was a hard time for you.'

'No sense running off to Darwin, though. Some no-good people hanging out there.'

Gradually the story emerged. Reading between the lines—more from what Nancy *didn't* say than from what she did—Elspeth got a clear glimpse of the sad picture. Turned upside down by a sense of grief and physical loss that she didn't fully understand, Nancy had made a blind bid for escape back into the world of near-homelessness and drug use she had first entered in Brisbane. It was a tragic variant on 'going walkabout', the restless urge that could grip Aboriginal people whose nomadic roots lay less than a generation away but who had lost too much of the culture in which that urge had its true place.

Arriving in Darwin, she had fallen in with a group of kids who were experienced in a destructive and deadly kind of abuse—petrol-sniffing. Apparently the Bradley boy who was now in prison had introduced her to it two years ago. She had kicked off this group and this habit after a few days, however, and had moved into a more sophisticated street culture where the drug was 'crack' a cheap, adulterated form of cocaine whose use was spreading across the Pacific from America.

Then something had sent out a warning signal to her. Perhaps it was simply that the burden of grief of the stillborn child had lifted, or perhaps it was something as small as the sores on her limbs which wouldn't heal. Whatever it was, she had been able to make the decision to return to Borragidgee and seek help.

'The trouble is,' Lachlan said later on in the afternoon, 'I'm not sure that we can justify keeping her in overnight for more than a couple of days. In a way it's a pity those sores weren't worse—callous and ironic though that sounds. We're not a rehabilitation centre, and she'll have some withdrawal symptoms. There will be days when she'll want to forget all this and try Darwin again. Still, we'll keep her in till Thursday. Perhaps we can even stretch it till the end of the week and meanwhile I'll put my mind to the problem.'

Annie arrived at that moment to report on the afternoon she had spent visiting local homes: one mother was using formula to feed her child and it wasn't working out, apparently. The baby seemed to be sick. Another woman had her arm in a home-made sling and wouldn't say what was wrong. Anne was afraid the arm might have been broken in a domestic fight and the woman was too frightened to seek treatment.

Lachlan took notes and made plans to check on a couple of cases himself, then he suddenly clapped an open hand to his forehead. 'Ellie, I said I'd meet the RFDS plane when it stops in from Darwin, and if I don't hurry I'll miss it.'

'If you want to finish with Annie, I'll go,' she answered quickly.

'Yes, could you?' He passed across the keys to the Toyota and she quickly drove out on the now-familiar road to the airstrip.

The plane was just taxiing to a halt when she arrived and Charlie's jeep from Walgunya was already waiting to pick up Uncle Bill. The middle-aged man greeted Ellie with a cheerful wave of his hand and she went to wait beside him, leaning, as he was, against the big metal roo bars across the front of the vehicle.

Two figures with dark faces against pale clothing emerged from the plane, which then taxied away to the end of the strip, ready to take off again since it still had one more medical stop to make before returning to base. As its passengers approached Ellie saw that they were both grinning, and she and Charlie grinned too at the sight of the almost identical white gauze dressings taped over each right eye. Little Andy was leading Uncle Bill by the hand, since he really was almost blind with just one filmed-over eye to see through.

The small boy began talking excitedly when he was still five yards off. 'He had a knife come right in his eye when it was open. He had a needle in up here so it didn't hurt, and I had that needle too, I did, the same.'

'Did you cry?' Elspeth teased gently, pretty sure of what the answer would be.

'Nope!' he said proudly.

'And Uncle Bill, how about you? Will you have the other eye done?'

'See if this one works properly first,' the old man said.

'Want a chocky biscuit?' Charlie said, holding out the packet he had concealed behind his back and chuckling as the old man's hand went unerringly to the right spot, beating Andy's quickly darted paw.

'I have to get back to the medical centre,' Elspeth said. 'But you both know when to come in and have your eyes looked at, don't you?' She repeated the instructions that would have been given at the hospital, and noted that Andy's left eye was already looking better since the erythromycin treatment had started.

The evening lay ahead. Elspeth faced it on the drive back to the medical centre with a nervousness and a pessimism that was becoming an everyday feeling. Jacqueline Harcourt hadn't been mentioned since

Saturday's dance, and yesterday had been spent around the house, cleaning and gardening. Lachlan had also shown Elspeth his collection of curios gathered in the spare-room, 'Since that'll make me tidy it up at last, and we can arrange your things better.'

The suggestion had been made in the slight gruff, shy way she had known in Darwin. It seemed to be a glimpse of what he had been like as a small boy, before his medical training and the love he had for his work had given him a deeper sense of confidence. Not that Ellie wanted to be married to a little boy. . . Lachlan's adult maleness was one of his most powerfully attractive attributes. But in those moments of shyness she discovered a new part of him to love, and felt herself being torn by pain and doubt inside once again. Could she go on like this, being fed crumbs when she needed and wanted the whole cake?

Perhaps Jackie would have dropped in to the medical centre. She did so a couple of times a week, usually at lunchtime or the end of the day, as if she wanted to be offered coffee or a drink—and Lachlan usually obliged her. The irritation and uneasiness Elspeth had felt in the past about these visits made sense now. If Jackie and Lachlan were secretly in love with each other, her own wariness was scarcely surprising. Subconsciously she must have been aware of what was going on well before it had clicked into place at Saturday's dance.

But what *was* 'going on'? With a cold thread of doubt running down her spine as she parked the Toyota in the driveway, Elspeth asked herself if Lachlan and Jackie could already be having an affair. She wouldn't be the first woman to share her husband with someone else less than six weeks after marriage, and, when the word 'love' had not been spoken between them, what certainty could she have about what he believed was right?

She sat in the driver's seat for ten long minutes, her

mind whirling with conflicting feelings and suspicions, then, shaking her head as if to physically force the thoughts aside, she went into the medical centre. Jackie wasn't there but Lachlan came through his office door and said immediately, 'I thought I heard the Toyota several minutes ago, and then you didn't come in. Is anything the matter?'

'No, I. . .was just being lazy,' she answered lamely, then added briskly, 'Andy and Uncle Bill are both fine. Is there anything else for me to do here, or shall I go and start dinner?'

The night passed and Lachlan spent it sleeping in the folding bed in the office area, within reach of Nancy who, he said the next morning, had woken several times, once thrashing and nearly hysterical after a nightmare. Elspeth couldn't help remembering how he had got one of the three health workers to sleep in the medical centre five weeks ago when Nancy was first here. Did he no longer think it worthwhile even to keep up the pretence that their married life was a normal, happy one?

The clinic day began with Annie's arival at the medical centre. Since she wasn't due to come in at all it was clear that something was up, but one or two darted sidelong glances from her at Elspeth prompted Lachlan to say, 'Let's go into my office and not disturb Ellie, since she had some paperwork.'

It was some fifteen minutes before the two of them emerged again, and Annie left straight away. A patient was already waiting, an older man from the newly developed Radnor mines who was worried about chest pain and wanted a thorough check-up, so the Aboriginal girl's visit went by without discussion between Ellie and Lachlan.

The day passed in a series of routine cases such as this first one, and it wasn't until three o'clock that Lachlan received a radio call to go up to the south boundary of

Walkadu Park where a camper had cut his foot on some broken glass and was unable to drive.

Their waiting-room was empty at the time so Lachlan said, 'If no one else has come by four you might as well shut up shop, as long as you stay around the house.'

'What about Nancy?'

'Florence is coming in at six, and Nancy can come through to the house if she needs anything before that. Leave the connecting doors unlocked, of course.'

'She's sleeping at the moment, as she did yesterday afternoon, so I doubt that she'll want me.'

'Annie told me something interesting this morning.'

'Oh, yes?'

'It looks as if there'll be a wedding soon between Florence's father and Nancy's aunt—but I must get going.' He had been collecting some extra medical equipment as he spoke, and was now ready to leave.

'We can talk about Nancy later,' Elspeth said.

'Bye, then.' Taking her by surprise, he planted a quick kiss on her lips. Instinctively her eyes closed and when she opened them again he was already out of the door and striding rapidly towards the Toyota. Helplessly she closed the door behind him.

It didn't seem fair that a quick peck like that could wreak such havoc on her peace of mind. With a firm effort of will, she started to think about the implications of a wedding between Lou Walpir and Harry Dixon. It could provide a solution, as it was likely that the three Walpir women would all move out to the Nagadi house where there would be plenty to occupy Nancy as well as Florence's presence as an encouraging example.

At four o'clock, Elspeth was just about to do as Lachlan had suggested and lock the main door of the medical centre when she heard the high roar of a vehicle outside, followed by an abrupt silence as its engine was switched off. She was becoming accustomed, by this time, to recognising visitors by the sound of their cars without looking from the window, and this didn't sound like Lachlan's Toyota. It was too early for him, in any case.

Then she heard Jackie Harcourt's voice outside, raised high with anxiety. 'Lachlan? Elspeth? Can you help me?'

In a moment Ellie was out of the door. The four-wheel-drive was parked at a crazy angle in the driveway as if the journalist had been in too much of a hurry to get it straight. She stood at the passenger door and was helping a small dark figure out on to the ground. Granny Alice Tirltirra.

The old woman gave some scolding whimpers and was clearly distressed. She took a few halting steps forward then staggered and almost collapsed, and Jackie's hold on the fragile elbow seemed stiff and inadequate.

There was a wheelchair in the store-room which fortunately Elspeth had not yet locked. She pulled it out hurriedly and grabbed some paper towelling to wipe it off a little, since it hadn't been used in a long time. The old woman slumped into it, more because her legs wouldn't hold her up than out of any realisation of what the chair was for, and Ellie wheeled her along the concrete path and—with difficulty—up the three wide steps into the medical centre. Jackie followed awkwardly only a few paces behind.

'What happened?' Ellie asked.

'It doesn't matter what happened,' Jacqueline snapped. 'Just do something for her.'

'If I don't know what happened, how on earth can I do anything for her?' Elspeth hit back, finding a shameful relief in being sharp with this woman.

'She fell over. It's quite simple.'

'How? To the right, or left, or——'

'Hell, Elspeth, I don't know. Left, I think. Just find out if she's broken anything. Is Lachlan here?'

'No. He won't be back for an hour at least.'

This news seemed to come as a relief to Jackie and she relaxed a little. 'She was. . .showing me over Walgunya a bit more and she fell down. I practically had to carry her back to the car. It was exhausting, and now she doesn't seem to know what's happening. I know old people have bones as brittle as chalk——'

'Yes, they often do,' Ellie said shortly. 'I thought Lachlan wasn't happy about you going out to Walgunya and spending time with Granny Alice.' As she spoke, she was coaxing and manoeuvring the old woman into position on the surgery table.

'She wanted me to,' Jackie answered defensively. 'She hasn't broken her hip or something has she?'

Elspeth gave no reply to this since she now had more important things to focus on. 'Does this hurt, Granny Alice?' she asked gently, beginning to massage and manipulate the limbs with practised hands as she searched for damage and assessed the range of motion and level of pain. From the way she had been trying to walk before slumping into the wheelchair, serious damage seemed unlikely.

But the old Aboriginal woman's moans could have meant pain or fear or simply confusion, and she was mumbling incoherently in her tribal tongue. Suddenly, Ellie remembered Nancy. 'Don't let her get off the bench,' she said to Jackie, and went down to where the sixteen-year-old lay dozing in the ward.

'Would you be able to help me, Nancy?' she said to the girl.

'Help you?' She sat up and pulled her cotton dress straight. She had been lying on top of the bed, not in it, and a magazine containing a cartoon comic strips slipped to the floor untidily. It wasn't a high-brow form of literature but it kept the girl occupied and she was already looking better than she had done yesterday.

'Yes, we have Granny Alice here and she's feeling very confused. She fell down and we want to find out if she's been hurt, but she won't respond when we speak English. If you could speak to her there's a better chance of getting through.'

'OK, all right, I'll talk to her.' Nancy scrambled from the bed, seeming quite keen on the idea of providing help, and Ellie suddenly wondered if this could be a way to anchor the girl in some useful activity. Would she possibly be able to train as a health worker?

It was a difficult twenty minutes and even Nancy, speaking in the tongue that Granny Alice had grown up with, took a while to get through. Jackie was worse than useless. She stood by, sharp-tongued and agitated, while Elspeth tried to find out if anything was broken. An X-ray would have been simpler but only Lachlan knew how to work the rather basic equipment, although he was planning to give her a lesson in its use soon. Dimly Elspeth thought that there was something odd about Jackie's appearance today, but didn't have time to work out what it was. Perhaps it was just that the journalist was more plainly dressed than usual, in old jeans and a long-sleeved cotton shirt.

Elspeth straightened up after examining Granny Alice as well as she could on the surgical table. 'We'll try to get her to walk now,' she said. 'I'm almost certain her pelvis and thigh-bones are completely intact, as well as her spine. She'd be in more pain otherwise. So you can be grateful for that, Jackie, because those are the places that really don't heal well at her age.'

'You needn't go on making me feel bad about this,' Jackie retorted coldly, and Ellie felt a little guilty.

'No, I'm sorry; I'm sure you're feeling bad enough on your own,' she said. 'Her left ankle is the main thing. It's looking badly swollen already and I think it might be broken. There's point tenderness and swelling around the——'

'That medical stuff makes no sense to me,' Jackie said, waving her hand dismissively.

'Well, anyway, I'll splint it temporarily, then Lachlan can X-ray it when he gets back.'

Jackie looked at Nancy uneasily then took a long breath and spoke. 'Look Elspeth, when he does come back would you mind leaving me out of this?'

'What do you mean, "leave you out"?'

'It's obvious, isn't it? Just don't tell him I was involved. Say that one of the Walgunya people brought her in. After all, she could have fallen like this any time.'

'I can't do that, Jackie,' Elspeth began slowly, then her head jerked on her neck as the journalist pulled her from the surgery and slammed the door on Nancy and Granny Alice.

'Don't make that self-righteous face,' she hissed, her blue eyes glittering coldly. 'I'm not asking you to lie. Don't be so petty. Whether she's got a broken ankle or just a sprain, it's hardly important who was with her at the time. I'm having enough trouble. . .with the book. . .and Lachlan and I. . .' She broke off and Elspeth suddenly saw with shocked surprise that she was crying, pressing a beringed hand stiffly to her face to conceal the blotchiness that was beginning to spread there.

For a moment Elspeth suspected that the tears were a bid to gain sympathy, then she saw that they were quite real and unplanned. She had not imagined that she would ever see the cool Englishwoman so upset, and felt pity for her. The shock of Granny Alice's fall and the long journey into town must have taken a heavy toll on Jackie's emotions.

'All right,' she said, watching as the tears slowly subsided and Jackie dived into a wad of paper tissues pulled from the pocket of her jeans. 'I won't tell Lachlan unless it comes up directly. As you suggested, I won't lie, but I'll gloss over the truth a little. I'm sure you'll want to tell him yourself in a few days when you're feeling better about it, and perhaps that's the best thing anyway. I'm not a tattletale.'

'Would it be all right if I go then? I'm feeling. . .well, exhausted, and I won't be fit to drive if I don't go soon.'

'Yes, go along then. We can radio Walgunya to send someone in for Granny Alice or we can run her home ourselves in the Toyota when Lachlan gets back. He may want to keep her in overnight, anyway.'

He did, arriving back after five-thirty and greeting the news of Granny Alice's fall with a frown. An X-ray revealed a fracture at the base of the fifth metatarsal. 'Did you get all the details?' he asked. 'Whoever brought her in didn't wait. Who was it?'

'I. . . I forgot to ask his name.' There! she had been forced to lie already. 'What details do you mean?'

'Was she alone when she fell? How near to the homestead? Did anyone see it happen or was she lying for some time waiting to be found?'

'I'm afraid I was so busy trying to get her safely inside to look at her, I forgot to ask.' This was partly true. She *didn't* know how far from the homestead Jackie and the old woman had been.

Lachlan shrugged tiredly. 'Well, I suppose it's not important for now. It's more a question of what's going to become of her when she goes back out there.'

'Will you keep her in here for long?'

'Just tonight. Of course we'll need to make sure she doesn't walk on it, but the Walgunya people will have to deal with that. She's the type that doesn't do well in this sort of environment. She needs her own place. But it's good that we have Nancy here, since she's so confused with her language at the moment.'

'Tell Nancy that,' Ellie said quickly. 'I think she'd be pleased.'

'Would she?' He gave her a look of sharp interest, and she didn't need to explain any further. He was thinking, as she had, that this might be a way through to Nancy.

Ellie watched Lachlan as he checked Granny Alice's hip and pelvic area one final time, asking questions about pain and giving instructions to the old woman through Nancy's interpretation, and coming to the same conclusions that Ellie had reached herself. There was full range of motion and no sign of tenderness so he decided against an X-ray of this area. Elspeth loved the shape of his face when it was focused on his work like this, the calmness of it, the intelligence in his eyes and the thoroughness revealed by the steady set of his closed mouth.

But the cover-up of Jackie's involvement in the old woman's accident weighed on her heavily, and she knew she wouldn't feel at ease with Lachlan until Jackie herself came to him with the story. It was the first piece of dishonesty between them—or the first piece on her part. She wondered again about her fear that Lachlan and Jackie might embark on an affair. Was that the reason why Jackie had been so reluctant for Lachlan to know? Was she afraid that it would put him off just when he was on the point of going to her?

Ellie remembered the sobbed phrase, 'Lachlan and I. . .' and felt sick with fear about the future. If Jackie didn't come out with the story herself by the end of the week she knew that she would have to be the one to explain, and would that just open up the whole can of worms? What else could it do?

CHAPTER TEN

IT WAS ten past eleven on Friday morning when Jackie came into the medical centre, and Lachlan had left just fifteen minutes before.

'Will he be back soon?' was one of the first things the journalist said, and Elspeth couldn't help wondering if she had been keeping an eye on the driveway at intervals that morning and had deliberately waited until the Toyota had disappeared.

But she answered Jackie innocently. 'Back soon? I'm no sure. Did you want to see him?'

'No! At least, I. . . Look at my arms and legs! I'm in pain and it's getting infected. I can't stand it any more.' She pushed up her loose left sleeve, and if she had been hoping for a dramatic moment she wasn't disappointed.

'My God, what have you *done*?' Ellie gasped.

Two raw red cuts ran for at least six inches along the inside of her forearm. They had the swollen, inflamed edges and yellowish ooze that showed infection, and there looked to be dirt in them as well. The only good thing that could be said about the cuts was that originally they had not been deep ones.

Now Jackie seemed to lose her taste for sensation. 'Don't fuss,' she said. 'This isn't the worst. It's all nothing and stupid. I'm sure it would get better if I left it, but then I started thinking about tetanus. Oh lord!'

'Come into the surgery, Jackie,' Ellie said, not without sympathy.

Again, as on Tuesday, the other woman seemed on the verge of tears. In fact. . .studying her made-up eyes more closely, Ellie wondered if she had been crying

172

already. Scarcely surprising if she had. With fingers that trembled and none of her usual poise, she slipped off her shirt and jeans to show lines of cuts on her lower legs and right arm as well, all of them puffy and weeping.

'This can't have been an accident,' Elspeth blurted. 'And it can't have happened today.'

'No, of course not. It was on Tuesday, with Granny Alice. It was a sacred rite. I was being initiated into the women's tribe.'

'*What*?' The door of the surgery, which had been slightly ajar, creaked on its hinges as it opened fully and Ellie felt a shiver run down her spine. Lachlan stood there. After that first angry and disbelieving word had broken from him, he was silent, his eyes fixed on Jackie as if he couldn't believe what he saw.

'You're back,' Jackie stammered.

'Yes, it was a bit of a false alarm. A fall in the school playground. The girl is fine now. *What is wrong with your arm*?'

'It was an initiation rite,' Jackie repeated with a defiant lift of her head, after clearing her throat and struggling to drop the whimpering tone she had used to Elspeth. 'My description of it will be the climax to the book and will hold the whole thing together. It all took place at the sacred women's site at Walgunya which Granny Alice showed me. It was on the way back that she fell down.'

'Ellie, you told me it was a man from Walgunya who brought the old lady in.'

Elspeth hesitated, waiting for Jackie to jump in and say that the cover-up was her fault, but the English journalist didn't speak, so in the end she said reluctantly, 'Jackie asked me not to tell you. She wanted to discuss it with you properly herself.'

'Look, is this important now?' Jackie put in impatiently. 'I'm here for treatment, not a lecture.'

'Why didn't you come in two days ago?' Lachlan asked.

He spoke in a controlled, quiet voice, but Ellie could see his anger. The three of them were alone in the medical centre. Elspeth herself had taken Granny Alice back to Walgunya on Wednesday morning and had given careful instructions to the people there about the old woman's treatment. One of the health workers would make frequent checks over the next few weeks to make sure Granny Alice was looking after the cast properly, not walking too much, and in no pain.

Nancy Walpir had been discharged yesterday and was 'staying with Florence for a while, at the Dixons'.' Lachlan and Ellie were both hoping that this could turn into a long-term arrangement. The girl was still having periods of drug withdrawal symptoms, but her own determination to shake off the influence of the past two years ran deep, and her dabbling with a variety of stimulants had at least prevented any one substance from taking too strong a hold.

Jackie's answer to Lachlan's question came after a groping pause. 'These initiation lines are supposed to form scars,' she said. 'I wasn't supposed to treat them or wash them. I was supposed to rub them with sand so that the lines became raised. It's an ancient ritual.'

'It's rubbish!' Lachlan exploded suddenly. 'There's nothing like that in the women's culture out at Walgunya. Sure, ritual scarring is done among the men in some areas but it's part of a huge set of tasks and tests involving hunting, learning of special stories, song-cycles and ceremonies. The women's rituals are different. This wasn't initiation. It takes years to earn that. This was something you've hotch-potched together out of your own reading because you wanted it for the book, and you pestered Granny Alice with it until she didn't know *what* you wanted!'

'That's not true! We found a real bond.'

'Annie came to see me on Monday morning to ask me to stop you from going out there again. Apparently, Granny Alice had been upset for hours after your last two visits.'

'Upset?'

'Yes, because in one of her confused periods she *did* show you a place that she regards as secret. She's not sure of her own memory any more and after your visits she thinks back and it's all hazy and she fears she's broken all sorts of taboos.'

'If she didn't want to show me, why didn't she simply——?'

'Don't give those innocent protestations, Jackie. By Tuesday you knew you weren't welcome and you managed to get Granny Alice off into the bush and then back here without anyone seeing you. You wouldn't have done that if you hadn't known the Walgunya people didn't want you.'

'I was sincere,' Jackie answered, her voice fogged and vinegary with tears now. 'I wanted to talk about Aboriginal rituals in my book in a way that would generate respect and interest in their culture. Don't accuse me of being a cynic. Perhaps I fooled myself, but I was quite sincere.'

'Perhaps you were. . .' He sighed heavily, then turned to the basin and began to wash his hands, lathering them with water and soap and reaching almost to the elbows. 'Let's have a look at this mess, then. I'll give you a course of antibiotic when we've finished. Ellie, can you get some dressings ready?'

'Yes, of course.' She began to prepare sterile dressing packs while Lachlan set to work on Jackie's arms, cleaning, draining and disinfecting the long shallow wounds as well as probing with tweezers for the pieces of gritty sand caught within the broken flesh. Jackie quickly went white, bit her lip and looked away, but made no sound of pain.

'What were they all done with?' Lachlan asked as he worked.

'An arrow head,' Jackie answered, drawing in a sharp breath as antiseptic stung into the deepest scratch. 'Made in the traditional way, but out of glass.'

'Glass?'

'Yes, and I sterilised it first in the flames of the fire.'

'At least you had the sense to do that.'

'And I did most of the cuts. Granny Alice didn't seem to be able to do it, or to understand, or something. Is tetanus a possibility?'

'You had a shot as soon as you arrived here, didn't you?'

'Yes.'

'Then you're all right. Was the sand you rubbed into them fairly clean?'

'I got it from the creek near my caravan, and rinsed it thoroughly with drinking water. Only once a day, Wednesday and Thursday.'

Elspeth remembered Jackie's long-sleeved shirt on Tuesday afternoon, and the teary, tetchy manner. The long cuts had been fresh then, and no doubt painful. It made sense of Jackie's difficulty in helping Granny Alice and her eagerness to get home afterwards.

'You didn't really want permanent raised scars, did you?' Lachlan was saying.

'No, I. . . Of course not. I just wanted to experience the ritual and what it all felt like. I would have started to wash it all properly today, but when it got infected I got scared and came to you. Will it scar? It won't, surely!'

'I can't promise that. But they're shallow. The scars will be light, flat ones and they'll fade as time goes by.'

Jackie was silent, and Elspeth saw that she was blinking back tears again, but when she spoke a few minutes later it was with defiant confidence. 'There's no way I'm leaving this out of the book, though. It was a valid insight into Granny Alice's experience and her culture, and I'm not going to deny the truth of what I felt.'

Lachlan, bandaging her arms, did not reply.

Jacqueline Harcourt left Borragidgee the following Tuesday. She came into the medical centre to say goodbye when, once again, Elspeth was alone there and Lachlan was away on call. This time it seemed her disappointment at missing him was sharp and real.

'But he said he'd be here, since it was clinic day!'

'He got called out to the Radnor mines unexpectedly,' Elspeth said. 'I'm afraid it happens.'

'One of the drawbacks of being a doctor, I suppose— or of being married to one.' The journalist simply shrugged casually but beneath the offhand manner she seemed tense, her feelings tightly held in.

Elspeth wanted to study her more closely but could not do so without seeming rude. Though there were no patients at the moment, there had been earlier, and she was still finishing off the resulting paperwork.

'Could you give him this?' Jackie said after a pause. She held out an envelope made of pale blue and quite expensive-looking paper.

Elspeth took it, murmured, 'Of course,' and put it on the corner of the desk where it wouldn't be mislaid or forgotten.

'It's just a goodbye card.' The words came hastily and awkwardly. 'Nothing important. Just to thank him for the help he's given me with the book.'

'Did you include your English address?' Ellie asked. 'I'm sure he'll want to keep in touch.' Actually, she very much hoped that he didn't and was hiding a profound relief that Jackie was leaving the town, but it was the polite thing to say. In any case, the fact that the journalist was leaving meant that there was no cause for this stupid jealousy, didn't it?

But Jackie shifted uncomfortably at Elspeth's question, looking quickly at the card and then away again. 'Oh. . .my address in England, did you say? It's. . .it's in the card.'

'Would you like to stay for a cup of tea?' Ellie offered, again wanting to do the polite thing. 'I don't think Lachlan will be back until this afternoon, but——'

'No, I must get going if I'm to reach Darwin by tonight, towing that slow caravan. I told the Winthrop Hotel I'd be checking in by eight.'

She left after a few more politenesses on either side, and the rest of the day passed uneventfully. Ellie forgot about the card on the corner of her desk but Lachlan saw it as soon as he came in, saving it to open later as a patient had just arrived. If he did open it later, Elspeth didn't see, and he had made no comment about it by the end of the working day.

'I'd better just listen in to the radio session,' he said as they were tidying up.

'I'll start dinner, then,' Elspeth replied with a nod.

It was a pattern they had fallen into before, and Ellie knew she would have felt at home with the domestic routine if only. . .if only he loved her. Not for the first time she was aware of the sharp difference it made. As she slipped a tuna casserole into the oven, thinking that he would appear through the door at any minute, she imagined how it would be if she could throw herself into his arms as she wanted to do, if she could feel his kiss and hear the words whispered in her ear: 'Now we can forget about everything else. . .we're alone. . . I love you.'

But it wouldn't happen. She knew that by this time. He would keep his distance, toss a salad perhaps, chat lightly about the day, and only later when they made love would she begin to feel a yearning closeness to him, a physical union that, unmatched by emotion on his part, was fast becoming unbearable.

The door opened and he entered as she had known he would. 'Ellie, I have to go to Darwin tonight.'

The lettuce she had just taken from the fridge fell from her fingers and rolled on the floor, its outer leaves bruised. He bent and picked it up quickly, placing it in the sink as if to get the stupid thing out of the way.

'Darwin? Tonight?' she could only echo blankly.

He looked restless and agitated. 'Yes, I've just heard from the hospital over the radio. There's an American passing through tomorrow—Gerald Paley—one of *the* experts on health problems in under-developed populations. I'm too out of touch here. I need that sort of contact. A mini-conference has been set up from nine until four tomorrow, and Dr Hassall at Royal Northern strongly advised me to be there.'

'If there's a conference, why wasn't it organised further in advance?' Elspeth said slowly.

'Because Dr Paley's in Australia on holiday. It was pure chance that Jerry Hassall met up with him and convinced him to give his time. I'll have to pack a sandwich and a thermos and drive up to Darwin tonight.'

'Tonight? By road? But——'

'I know. It's a seven-hour trip,' he shrugged impatiently. 'There seems to be no choice, though. Jim Partridge is lending me his car so you can have the Toyota.' Clearly, it was all arranged. 'We must put in a request form for a second vehicle here. If I'd thought about it before you sold you car in Darwin. . .'

'How long will you be gone?' Ellie asked, hearing her own voice thin and reedy in her ears. It was terrible the way she needed him, needed even the unsatisfying companionship that was so much less than what she really wanted. 'If there's an emergency——'

'The Flying Doctor will have to be called, unless it's a minor thing you can deal with yourself. Jerry Hassall's organised all that. I'll be gone for two nights. Jerry is making a booking for me at the Winthrop Hotel. I'd better throw a few things together.'

He left the room with impatient strides and Ellie stood at the sink, the round ball of lettuce blurring in front of her eyes. Jackie's departure this morning. . .a mini-conference at short notice. . .the Winthrop Hotel. Feeling sick to her stomach, she thought, I don't believe him. What's wrong with me? What's wrong with *him*?

Jackie's card. Had he read it just then while waiting for the radio session to begin? Had it pleaded for an assignation in Darwin, and had he decided to go? I have to confront him with it. The idea whirled in her mind, not grounded in reality. Before she had touched the lettuce again—what was this meal for anyway, since he wouldn't be here to eat it?—Lachlan had re-entered the room, dumping a black vinyl overnight bag on the floor.

'Did you put the kettle on?'

'No, why. . . I. . .?'

'I thought you might have. Never mind. Five more minutes won't matter.'

He filled the electric kettle and plugged it in, then took slices of bread and cold meat, spread them with mustard and added lettuce leaves from the bruised head that she had finally managed to wash and squeeze dry. If he noticed her clumsiness and her silence, he said nothing about them.

She knew she should speak, bring the thing out into the open, but words would not come. It was as if her tongue and brain were both coated with wool. Erratically the thoughts formed themselves. If it's true that he's going to Jackie, then I can't bear to know. Not yet. If it isn't true and I accuse him of it, then he'll see right through me and pity me because of this stupid, jealous love—that he doesn't share.

When he left ten minutes later, she had said nothing. He would be back on Thursday, he had said, as early as possible. His kiss was awkward, mechanical, not hinting at desire, and it left her lips dry.

Numbly she prepared a small salad and ate some of the casserole. The rest would do for tomorrow night's meal when she would also be alone. Then on Thursday, when he returned, she would find a way to talk to him. It had to come out in the open now. They couldn't go on like this.

It occurred to her that if he *had* gone to Jackie tonight she might not need to bring the subject up herself. He might do it, returning from Darwin with a request to end their short, ill-conceived marriage so that he and Jackie could be free. His anger with the journalist had been real last week. Theirs would be a stormy relationship, but some people sought that and wanted it. Kate and John Dane still argued fiercely, and it didn't dampen their joy in each other and in their coming child.

It seemed that these pointless, repetitive thoughts did not stop even in sleep, and when she woke on Thursday morning Elspeth felt stiff, headachy and unrefreshed. Today was the final day of her immunisation round, so she took her gear shortly after breakfast, as she had done yesterday, and set off in the medical centre's Toyota. There weren't many places left to do this morning. She should be finished by lunchtime, and perhaps then she'd be able to take a nap to restore her energy before Lachlan returned.

In fact, she had showered and put on her red jersey dress, blow-dried her freshly washed hair and it was four o'clock before she heard the sound of Jim Partridge's car in the driveway. Heart thudding, she went out to meet

Lachlan, unable to bear the helplessness of waiting dumbly in the lounge-room for his appearance through the door.

He swept her into his arms with a muttered, 'God, that's a long drive!' and weakly she let herself fall against him, feeling his hard length through the softly draped folds of her open-necked dress and tingling as always at the caress of his hands over her back. His mouth came to hers hungrily and she tasted the dryness of the desert until their lips blurred together and became sweetly, gently moist.

'You smell delicious,' he said after a long moment.

'I just had a shower.'

'But you always smell delicious.'

'No, Lachlan. . .' Finding her strength and resolution at last, she pulled away and turned back towards the house. She half-expected him to reach for her again, but he didn't. Instead, as she walked up the path to the door—noting stupidly that the oleanders were sprouting some new shoots—she heard him open the car rear door of the vehicle and pull out his overnight bag, then begin to follow her towards the house.

She faced him as soon as they entered the lounge. 'Did you see Jackie in Darwin?'

'Yes, as a matter of fact, I did.' He looked embarrassed and his eyes skated away from any meeting with her own.

'And what happened?'

'Happened?' Again he looked embarrassed. 'Nothing happened.'

'Please. . .' She took an agonised step towards him and her voice broke on the word. 'Whatever you do or say, don't lie to me!'

He engulfed her then and her body shook against his as she sobbed, unable to speak. His own words came as whispers, tumbling against each other. 'Ellie, Ellie, my darling, what's the matter? Don't cry! I can't bear to see you like this without knowing what's wrong. What's happened?'

'You and Jackie. . .' she managed at last, barely taking in what he had said. 'You went to meet her in Darwin. She asked you to in that card and you went. If you want to be with her, if you want a divorce, tell me now. At least give me a chance to stop loving you before I wreck myself.'

'Stop loving me?' He held her so that her face was only inches from his. 'The last thing in the world I want you to do is to stop loving me. How could I let you do that when loving you is the most important thing in my life?'

'Why are you saying that?' she whispered.

'Because it's true.'

'You've never said it.'

'I know. Can I say it now?'

'Oh, say it all you like!' Laughter mingled with the tears that had been sparkling on her cheeks. Her shining hair fell over her forehead and he brushed it back, touching her lips to her face in a dozen places and whispering the words she had been waiting for so many weeks to hear. Then he pulled back a little.

'I was engaged once,' he said. 'It's been six years since it was broken off. The last time I said, "I love you" was the week before she sent back the ring and told me she was going to marry some stock-market whiz-kid. She liked his ambitions a lot better than mine.' There was a typical Scottish irony in the mild sentence. 'The pain of all that went away years ago, but I never lost the fear——'

'The fear of saying it?'

'Of making myself that vulnerable. I loved you from the minute I saw you in the Rock Bar in Darwin. At least, perhaps it's not love, that first feeling, but recognition. I just knew. . . And then I made that absurd proposal. . .it seemed impossible that you had said yes. . . I couldn't talk about love and you didn't either. You seemed happy to call it a practical arrangement so I tried to keep on treating it like that.'

'There have been lots of times when it *hasn't* been practical. . .'

'I know. Together, with nothing separating us at night, I couldn't hide how I felt, but you never spoke about it. I was afraid that for you it was just a physical release.'

'We've been feeling all the same things. It's so stupid,' Ellie laughed on a trembling note. 'But. . . I don't understand about Jackie.'

'You thought I was in love with her?'

'You always seemed interested in her, and so enthusiastic about her book.'

'I was trying to minimise the damage she did with it. I thought if I alienated her, if the town did, the sweeping statements and over-dramatisation and false analyses would only be worse, so I tried to be as friendly as I could. Well, it seems it wasn't the right approach, and it ended in a very embarrassing way.'

'How do you mean?'

'She *did* ask me to meet her in Darwin. When Jerry Hassall rang to tell me about the conference he suggested the Winthrop, since that was where the conference was being held, and I forgot that Jackie had said she'd be there. Actually, I skimmed that last part of the card. I felt so uncomfortable about what she was saying.'

'And then in Darwin. . .?'

'I ran into her by chance. She thought I'd come to tell her I loved her and that my marriage to you was over. I didn't want to tell you because it seemed unfair to her. We had an awful, awkward scene in her room, but I don't think she's permanently hurt. It seems there's someone in England whom she was unsure about when she left, and I imagine the idea of home is much rosier for her now. Probably my English connection is partly what attracted her. She's going home in a week to write the final draft of the book and work on the photographs. And as for what we're going to do. . .'

He released her and went to his bag. She watched him open the zipped side-compartment, his back strong and broad as he bent over it. Unable to stop herself, she took a step towards him and touched his neck with a gentle palm, just where the dark and slightly curly hair gave way to bare, tanned skin. She had the confidence to touch him now without waiting for darkness, and the right to be in his arms that came from shared, spoken love and nothing else.

'I did two silly things in Darwin,' he said, holding out two airline tickets. 'I booked us for a three-week trip to Bali next month. Don't you think we're ready for a honeymoon?'

'We'd start it now if I had three wishes,' Ellie whispered against his cheek. 'Bali!'

'I love you in this dress,' was his irrelevant answer. 'But would you be insulted if I said I wished you'd take it off?'

There was a knock at the door just then, and it could not be ignored. Lachlan's impatient pull on the handle revealed Greg Wirragurr, Borragidgee's part-time postman. It was mail day, and the plane would have dropped the bag off at the airstrip that morning.

'Coupla' letters,' he said, then left after Lachlan's friendly nod and greeting.

'Is this for me?' Ellie asked, seeing the hand-addressed white envelope on top. 'Wait a minute, this is *your* writing!'

'I know. That was the other silly thing. I wrote it in

Darwin as soon as I arrived and posted it first thing yesterday,' he said with a wry grin. 'I knew I'd get here before it did—in fact it's done the trip faster than I thought—but I was missing you so badly I just couldn't help it.'

'You can't have had a lot of news,' Ellie pointed out drily, trying to shrink away a delicious smile. 'What does it say?'

'Oh. . .one or two rather soppy things,' he said, shrugging, his Scottish drawl strong and slow. 'Don't read it.'

'Don't read it?'

'Can't I just say them in your ear. . .like this. . .instead?'

By the time he had finished they were somehow in the bedroom, and the red jersey dress was nowhere to be seen.

— MEDICAL  ROMANCE —

The books for your enjoyment this month are:

CARIBBEAN TEMPTATION Jenny Ashe
A PRACTICAL MARRIAGE Lilian Darcy
AN UNEXPECTED AFFAIR Laura MacDonald
SURGEON'S DAUGHTER Drusilla Douglas

♥ ♥ ♥ ♥ ♥

Treats in store!

Watch next month for the following absorbing stories:

HEART SEARCHING Sara Burton
DOCTOR TRANSFORMED Marion Lennox
LOVING CARE Margaret Barker
LOVE YOUR NEIGHBOUR Clare Lavenham

Available from Boots, Martins, John Menzies, W.H. Smith, Woolworths and other paperback stockists.

Also available from Mills and Boon Reader Service, P.O. Box 236, Thornton Road, Croydon, Surrey CR9 3RU.

Readers in South Africa — write to:
Independent Book Services Pty, Postbag X3010, Randburg, 2125, S. Africa.

Three women, three loves . . . Haunted by one dark, forbidden secret.

ALIX ATKINSON

Boundaries

Margaret – a corner of her heart would always remain Karl's, but now she had to reveal the secrets of their passion which still had the power to haunt and disturb.

Miriam – the child of that forbidden love, hurt by her mother's little love for her, had been seduced by Israel's magic and the love of a special man.

Hannah – blonde and delicate, was the child of that love and in her blue eyes, Margaret could again see Karl.

It was for the girl's sake that the truth had to be told, for only by confessing the secrets of the past could Margaret give Hannah hope for the future.

W●RLDWIDE

Price: £3.99   Published: April 1991

Available from Boots, Martins, John Menzies, W.H. Smith, Woolworths and other paperback stockists.

Also available from Mills and Boon Reader Service, P.O. Box 236, Thornton Road, Croydon, Surrey CR9 3RU

4 MEDICAL ROMANCES
AND 2 FREE GIFTS
From Mills & Boon

Capture all the excitement, intrigue and emotion of the busy medical world by accepting four FREE Medical Romances, plus a FREE cuddly teddy and special mystery gift. Then if you choose, go on to enjoy 4 more exciting Medical Romances every month! Send the coupon below at once to:

**MILLS & BOON READER SERVICE, FREEPOST
PO BOX 236, CROYDON, SURREY CR9 9EL.**
No stamp required

- ✂ - ✂ -

YES! Please rush me my 4 Free Medical Romances and 2 Free Gifts! Please also reserve me a Reader Service Subscription. If I decide to subscribe, I can look forward to receiving 4 Medical Romances every month for just £5.80 delivered direct to my door. Post and packing is free, and there's a free Mills & Boon Newsletter. If I choose not to subscribe I shall write to you within 10 days – I can keep the books and gifts whatever I decide. I can cancel or suspend my subscription at any time. I am over 18.

EP02D

Name (Mr/Mrs/Ms) —————————————————————

Address ——————————————————————————

————————————————————————————————

————————————————————— Postcode —————————

Signature ——————————————————————————